Angels of the Third Reich

by
Peter Alden Nerber

Copyright © 2020 Peter Alden Nerber
Polliwog Pages Publishing
All rights reserved.
(ISBN 9798671183931)

Contents

Book One

Angels of the Third Reich: He That Overcometh

Chapter 1	The Beginning of Sorrows	8
Chapter 2	The Comforted Abound	21
Chapter 3	A Meeting at Dachau	31
Chapter 4	The Road to Heaven	42
Chapter 5	The Visitors	48

Book Two

Angels of the Third Reich: Songs in the Night

Chapter 1	A Storm Approaches	58
Chapter 2	The Arrests	70
Chapter 3	Passing All Understanding	106
Chapter 4	To Be With Christ Is Far Better	111

Book Three

Angels of the Third Reich: Songs in the Night II

Chapter 1	The Assignment	122
Chapter 2	The Second Seal	130
Chapter 3	The Furnace of Affliction	136
Chapter 4	Martin's Homegoing	146

Book Four

Angels of the Third Reich: Belgium Resistance

Chapter 1	Andrew Heiden's Home-going	156
Chapter 2	God's Messengers	162
Chapter 3	Songs from Heaven	166
Chapter 4	Wola Massacre	177
Chapter 5	Resistance Fighters	181
Chapter 6	It Is Finished	190

ANGELS OF THE THIRD REICH: HE THAT OVERCOMETH

BOOK ONE

Mandlestrasse, 43, apt. 32a
Nazis besetzten München, Deutschland
September, 1941

Chapter 1

THE BEGINNING OF SORROWS

"All these are the beginning of sorrows. Then shall they deliver you up to be afflicted, and shall kill you: and ye shall be hated of all nations for my name's sake. And then shall many be offended, and shall betray one another, and shall hate one another." (Matthew 24:8-10)

Agnes Weiss, an eighteen-year old, had been a student at Europe's most prestigious University of Munich. She laid her book down on the coffee table, walked to the window to see what was happening. She called into the other room to her brother, Hanz. "Hey, there's something going on outside the Heisler's bakery."

"Oh, I'm sure there is, Agnes. I spoke to him yesterday. He told me he was going to start speaking out against the Nazis. I warned him against it, but he said he'd already made up his mind."

Ezra Heisler was the owner of Heisler's Jewish Bakery. The Weiss family and the Heislers had been friends for as long as Agnes could remember.

An SS officer, (Schutzafell, an elite organization within the Nazi Party) was shouting and soon began slapping Herr Heisler around, uttering oaths and racial slurs. Two Munich police officers sporting swastika armbands soon entered the picture. They approached the SS officer who muttered an order. The Munich police officers entered the back room of the bakery and soon appeared in the window. One of them held up an ornate box. The SS officer nodded and motioned for the box to be brought to him. Upon opening it, he shouted an oath. The box contained a yellow star. He held it up to Heisler's face. He pushed him against the brick storefront and continued shouting.

Heisler, an old man, began shouting angrily at the officer. Agnes was surprised at the volume of Heisler's voice, for a man his age. She could clearly hear everything he was saying.

The officer told him to shut up and then delivered several heavy punches to his stomach.

Heisler cried out and collapsed from the pain. "*Bo Ruach Elohim Adonai!*" ("Come, O Spirit of God!")

The invocation further angered the officer. He unclipped his 9mm Luger and leveled it at Heisler's forehead, demanding that he shut up.

Agnes gasped, realizing what she was about to witness.

Heisler cried out again, "*Elohim Rahman! Elohim Rahman!"* ("God have mercy on me, God have mercy on me!") He held up his quivering hands as if to shield himself from the inevitable.

The officer threw his head back and laughed like a hound from hell. He said, "My God, the suspense is too much for me!" The terrible crack and thud of the bullet hitting its target point blank came a second later. It was instantly followed by a massive bright red mist that covered the wall and window behind the slumped Herr Heisler, whose hands were still quivering of their own accord.

Heisler's sons, Abraham and Jacob, were enraged and would have killed the officer. The officer quickly defused the rage by pulling his dagger and pressing it against Jacob's throat. He said, "Don't start anything. You are not on the list . . . yet. Understood?" The young men nodded. "Clean the wall and get the body off the street. NOW!" he demanded.

The young men scurried to do the officer's command. Jacob muttered a vulgar, *"Goyim Bastard!"* as he scrubbed the wall.

"What did you say, Jewish swine?!"

"You heard me!" He rose and spit in the officer's face. The furious officer reeled and wiped his face and glasses, then struck Jacob hard with his crop. The blow caught Jacob off balance, but he quickly composed himself and continued cleaning. O*h, it was so worth the pain*, he thought.

"Clean the wall! Clean the window! You filth! Clean it up!" shouted the officer. He then chuckled and walked away.

"Abraham, get me some more towels and let's get this cleaned up," said Jacob. When they finished they went inside to try to comfort their mother.

The aged Frau Heisler sat wailing in the living quarters above the store. Her screams echoed up and down the street like something from a nightmare.

Tears filled Agnes' eyes as she sobbed. She had lost a dear friend. Herr Heisler. He had been like a grandfather to her. The whole scene was surreal. It was difficult to absorb as being reality. *How could this happen?*

Agnes looked away from the window for no more than a second to get a handkerchief from her pocket. When she looked again at the scene below, she was shocked to see two well-dressed gentlemen in their middle thirties, kneeling on either side of Heisler's body. They were noticeably much taller than the old man. One had wavy blond hair. The other had light brown hair. A shaft of golden light shone around them, reflecting on their shoulders.

One of them looked directly up at Agnes. The heavenly kindness that enveloped him took Agnes's breath away. She watched as they helped the old man to his feet and began to walk down the street and then vanished. It was hard to believe, but she knew she had just seen two angels of death come for her friend. At least now, she thought, he was no longer the subject of hatred, as were hundreds of other Jews throughout the city.

And it came to pass, that the beggar died, and was carried by the angels into Abraham's bosom" (Luke 16:22)

The Reich had recently passed a law which required all Jews over the age of six throughout the Nazi occupied countries to wear an armband with the Star of David, and the word "Jude" (Jew) stitched inside the star. All those who refused to wear this star ran the risk of being shot. Agnes suspected that Herr Heisler, being a man proud of his Jewish heritage, would not wear his armband. That was the item the police found in the ornate box.

Agnes walked to the doorway of the next room, tears still streaking her face. "We've got to do something for them, brother. He did nothing wrong. He was just an innocent shopkeeper trying to provide for his family."

"I heard the shouting and the gunshot. But was he wearing his star?" asked Hanz.

"No. But why would that have made a difference?"

"It's cruel, I know, but Hitler is a beast. In order to survive his reign of terror, you have to comply with his rules. If Heisler refused to wear the star and spoke out, he pretty much signed his own death warrant."

"But there must be something we can do."

"Look, the Gestapo is everywhere. Every block has informants. I even heard that Frau Braun was arrested last week for feeding a Jewish woman and her children. Frau Braun's own children were the ones who turned her in. She was sent to Ravensbruck the next day, and the children are now property of the State. You can't even trust your own children nowadays."

"A man's foes shall be they of his own household."
(Matthew 10:36)

"I'm going to see if Frau Heisler needs anything," said Agnes.

"Agnes, did you not hear what I just told you? You cannot be caught helping a Jew."

"Then I won't get caught." Agnes paused for a moment, thinking about how to phrase the next thing she wanted to say. "I know the risks. Really, I do. But there comes a time when we put aside even our own lives for the sake of others, for those who have no one to speak out in their defense."

That evening at dinner, Hanz remembered a verse he had heard when he was young. Their mother regularly took Hanz and Agnes to a Greek Orthodox church. One Sunday morning at church, the minister had based his sermon on John 21:17. *"He saith unto him the third time, Simon, son of Jonas, lovest thou me?"* Peter was grieved because he said unto him the third time, *"Lovest thou me?"* And he said unto him, Lord, thou knowest all things; thou knowest that I love thee." *Jesus saith unto him, "Feed my sheep."* Hanz was overwhelmed how this verse came to him at the same time he was struggling about helping his Jewish friends.

From that day on, Agnes and Hanz did everything they could for the Heislers, and anyone else who came to their door for help. They had to be very careful not to be seen by the SS or someone who might be working for the Gestapo.

This was difficult, since anyone could be working for them in one way or another.

Hanz and Agnes were constantly looking over their shoulder, now that they were knowingly breaking the laws of the Reich concerning the Jews. Since their decision to resist, they were nervous around all law enforcement in Munich. Even the police they had grown up with, and viewed as friends, could not be trusted, as the police was heavily controlled by the Nazis. The mere sight of a uniform gripped them with fear.

The stress began to cause health issues. Often Hanz and Agnes felt their hearts pounding. They also found themselves praying more. The Christian faith they had grown up with as children became very important to them. It was now a sort of haven into which they could retire if they felt alone after working long days in the munitions factory.

On her way home Saturday evening, Agnes took a shortcut from the main street to her apartment building. She passed a small boy curled up against one of the tall brick buildings. His face was buried in his hands and he sobbed quietly. She paused down the alley and looked back at the boy. His clothes were filthy and torn, and his body was covered in cuts and bruises.

A minister from the Greek Orthodox church came down the alley but passed by on the opposite side when he saw the boy. In a few moments, a deacon from the church also came down the alley. He paused and walked over to the boy and looked at him. When he noticed the yellow star on his torn shirt, he went on his way. A one armed old veteran of the German Revolution also passed. Scowling and jeering as he passed, he grumbled, "*Judenschwein!*" ("Jewish Pig!") "Do you think I fought in the Revolution so you could be free to leech off of society?"

Agnes was brought to tears as she watched the scene unfold. No one would help the boy. He was all alone in the world, forsaken by his fellow countrymen because they were caught up in the political frenzy. Most of whom never stopped to consider why this persecution was happening to the Jews.

Agnes saw the modern equivalent of the story Jesus gave in Luke 10:30-32, about the Jewish man who came down from Jerusalem to Jericho. He fell among thieves who beat him and tore his clothes, taking what little he had. Many passed by, but none offered to help him. She knew she had no choice but to finish the passage set before her: *"But a certain Samaritan, as he journeyed, came where he was: and when he saw him, he had compassion on him."* (Luke 10:33)

Approaching the boy cautiously, she knelt beside him, putting a hand on his shoulder. *"Shalom,"* she addressed him kindly.

The boy looked up warily and whispered, "*Shalom* . . . I am a Jew."

She felt hurt deeply in her heart. He spoke to her in the way a leper would in ancient Jerusalem to warn people not to come too close. The boy was not more than twelve years of age, and already knew full well the feelings of rejection, fear and utter loneliness. Indeed, he was a political leper, one of whom the world was not worthy.

Agnes said, "So? I am a Christian. It makes no difference. We are all of the same blood created by God."

"Germans aren't supposed to help Jews."

"I . . ." she lacked the words to say. The comment cut to her very core. "Are you hungry?" The boy nodded. It was dark, and the back streets had grown silent. "Come with me to my apartment. We will take care of you."

"You'll be in trouble."

Agnes sighed quietly and said, "I'm already in a lot of trouble, brother. It's not important now. Will you come?"

The boy, overwhelmed by her kindness, reached up and hugged her tightly. She returned the gesture and prayed for their safety. If they were caught, she knew they would die.

"For I was an hungred, and ye gave me meat: I was thirty, and ye gave me drink: I was a stranger, and ye took me in." (Matthew 25:35)

A recent notice had been posted on every public building in Nazi occupied countries warning people not to help the Jews. It bore a chilling text which read:

Notice: Concerning the Sheltering of Escaping Jews:

There is a need for a reminder, that in accordance with paragraph 3 of the decree October 15, 1941, on the limitation of residence in general government (page 595 of the G.G. register) Jews leaving the Jewish quarter without permission will incur the death penalty.

According to this decree, those knowingly helping these Jews by providing shelter, supplying food or selling them foodstuffs are also subject to the death penalty. This is a categorical warning to the non-Jewish population against:
1) <u>Providing shelter to Jews,</u>
2) <u>Supplying them with food</u>
3) <u>Selling them foodstuffs</u>

TschenstochauCzęstochowa 24.9.42
Der Stadthauptmann Dr.Frank (City Governor)

Though such a decision may cost her life, Agnes believed she had no choice. She had been given this clear visual prodding, and she dared not brush it aside. She hoped no one saw her as she hurried to the apartment building and up the three flights of stairs. "Hurry!" she urged him, "We're almost there." Her heart was pounding. She gave a sigh of relief as they went inside and closed the door.

"What have you done, Agnes?!" Hanz asked. He could hardly believe he was seeing a Jewish boy standing in the room.

"He fell among thieves. He was beaten and his clothes were torn. I thought he could stay here for a few days."

Hanz turned to the boy. "Make yourself at home my friend . . . just stay away from the windows, understand?"

The boy nodded. He said his name was Aaron.

Hanz pulled Agnes aside into the sitting room. "What are you doing!" His voice was both angry and fearful. "Helping a Jewish family we've known for years is one thing. But hiding Jews—that is taking breaking the law to a whole different level."

"Hanz, we are already in trouble by helping the Heislers. What difference does it make now? He's an orphan. He has nothing. No one in this world cares about him."

"What if someone saw you? You had to climb three flights of stairs."

"No one saw me. It's September, Hanz. The nights are getting cold. He wouldn't have lasted another week in his condition." She paused for a moment and then said, "Jesus taught us that if we see a person in need of food and clothes and we refuse to help, it's as if we refused to help Jesus himself if He needed help."

Hanz nodded and sighed. "All right. We'll do it your way."

They returned to the living room and found the boy fast asleep on the sofa. Hanz began to quote the rest of the story in Luke 10:34: *"And he went to him, and bound up his wounds, pouring in oil and wine . . . and brought him to the inn, and took care of him."*

"There's more to that," said Agnes. "Jesus said in verse 37 '*Go, and do thou likewise.*'"

"Well, in that case, let us trust God to help us overcome what may be ahead and do His bidding, and only for His glory.

Chapter 2

THE COMFORTED ABOUND

One evening, Hanz called his sister into the study. He was seated by his favorite window on the south side of the room. A Bible lay open on the stand beside him. "Agnes, look at this." Hanz pointed to the underlined passage and read aloud, "*Let us therefore come boldly unto the throne of grace, that we may obtain mercy, and find grace to help in time of need.*" (Hebrews 4:16)

Agnes read the verse again to herself.

"What do you think of that?" asked Hanz.

"We should pray as if we were literally inside the courts of heaven, surrounded by the saints and angels," answered Agnes.

"Sometimes on my way home from the factory, I would feel like someone is following me, so I'd pray and get a comforting feeling of warmth and safety that I couldn't explain," said Hanz.

"Well, Hanz, we need as much protection as we can get now that we are intentionally breaking the law."

Hanz paused for a moment, being careful how he told his sister about the postcard he had received in the post the day before. "Take a seat, Agnes. There is something I want you to read. This postcard came yesterday."

Agnes read it and sat on the couch. Her best friend, Sophia Reinstein had been shipped to the concentration camp at Treblinka, in Eastern Poland. The postcard had been sent from the camp, saying she had arrived there safely. She encouraged Hanz and Agnes to move closer to her, into Eastern Poland. Everything about the postcard screamed "PHONEY!"

"Hanz, there seems to be something written between the lines." Agnes retrieved a magnifying glass from the desk and slowly moved the postcard under the glass. Between the lines, was a separate message altogether. It was written with something like a sharp pointed stick, for the words were indented on the postcard, and not visible to the naked eye.

"*Dear Agnes, Ninety percent of the women and all the children are sent to the gas chambers. I risk my life in giving you this report. I am working at the seamstress shop now, but I do not expect to live long. Goodbye, my dear friend. Love, Sophia"*

"Well, what did it say?" asked Hanz.

"Umm, she's working at the seamstress shop right now, but most of the people who come through there are sent to the gas chambers. We really should try t—" She was cut off by a knock on the door. "Who could that be at this time of night?"

"I don't know. I'll get the door," replied Hanz.

Two men wearing leather overcoats and wool fedoras stood at the door. They were Gestapo agents. Hanz's and Agnes's test of faith had begun.

"Are you Hanz Weiss?" asked the taller of the two.

"Yes. I am Hanz Weiss. Who are you?"

This agent nodded to the other. The other agent then punched Hans hard in the stomach. Hanz doubled over in pain and collapsed on the floor.

"God help me!" he cried out, gasping for breath.

"You ask too many questions. Now shut up!"

He took Hanz by the arm and pulled him up.

Agnes came running in. "What are you doing!"

"Just bringing him for questioning. It won't take long, Fraulein. He'll be back in a few hours. Don't worry about him." His voice was sinister. His face thin and pale, but neat and clean, like a well-kept grave. His eyes were ice blue but had no bright gleam like many Germans his age. His eyes were like those of a beast of prey: cold, concentrated, and focused on only one thing: to devour his catch.

"But what's his crime?" Agnes persisted. "What has he done?"

The men paused for a moment. The tall one shrugged and replied, "Who knows? I just follow orders." He chuckled nervously and left with Hanz.

A few minutes later, the agents came to the intersection of Briennerstrasse and Turkmenstrasse. At the northeast corner of these two streets stood a massive

Romanesque-style building, Wittelsbacker Palace built by the German architect Friedrich Von Gartner in 1843. The Gestapo had claimed it for their headquarters in 1933. Since then the residents of Munich dared not speak out against Hitler's atrocities. Anyone who resisted the rules and regulations of the Reich would be taken to the headquarters and subject to violence, grueling interrogation, and possibly death.

The car stopped at the front door of the Palace. Hanz was roughly pushed out of the back seat and taken inside the building. He was promptly taken below the main office space to a five by five cell, which was pitch black and very cold. In one corner there was a low cot for a prisoner to sleep. He knelt and felt the floor. It was made of rough cement.

After two hours had passed, he was beginning to experience the effects of sensory deprivation. This technique was used during the war on both sides for successful interrogation of prisoners. The Gestapo was already trying to break him, and it was starting to work. He asked himself if he would be able to withstand what might come next. He prayed as he knelt on the floor. "Father in Heaven," he whispered, "You know my weakness. Give me the right words to say and give me strength to endure. Whatever may happen tonight, you are my comfort and strength. You are my high tower in which I may always find refuge. Amen."

Then the interrogation began. Two men escorted Hanz to a small room at the end of a hall on the second floor. A small sign above the door read: *Verhor* (Interrogation) Three hours of psychological and physical torture and endless questions followed. Somehow, he endured.

The Gestapo agent who conducted the interrogation asked strange questions, to which Hanz had difficulty answering. Every time he didn't answer to the agent's satisfaction, a large man in a plain business suit would grip his powerful hands onto Hans' tricep pressure point, making him cry out in agony.

"I am sorry, you know. I don't like hurting people, but you must learn to comply with our rules and not lie to me. I really hate that. This room is sound-proofed. You can scream as much as you want. It's a natural reaction when the nerves don't know what to do with that kind of pain." Finally, he closed the file and said, "That's all. You can go home for now. I would advise you not to speak of this to anyone, otherwise you will disappear in the middle of the night."

As Hanz left, he looked at his watch. 12:30 A.M. He was exhausted. He pressed his fingers gently into his eyes. They burned from having been taken from a room void of any light into a room with a bright bulb that hung directly above him. Blood filled his nostrils and he was shaking from the emotional strain. The bleeding stopped quickly. The night air was refreshing. As he walked, he thought about the events that preceded. He was usually a lad of weak emotional endurance, but he had suffered three hours of professional psychological and physical abuse, and he had been released. He began to smile. He felt comforted that his simple prayer was answered in a beautiful way. His strength was not his own.

As he rounded the last block before Mandlestrasse, an authoritative voice addressed him from the darkness of the alley. "Hanz Weiss?" A tall young man emerged into the light. He wore a spotless white business suit. "Don't be afraid, Weiss. I am a friend. My name is Ariel."

"How did you know my name?" Hanz asked, studying the stranger.

He replied, "I knew your father shortly before he was killed."

The comment stunned Hanz. "W-were you in the war?"

"In a way. I was there to help people cross into their heavenly home."

Hanz remembered the letter in a box of his father's personal effects that was written as he lay dying. In it, he made mention of a "*Kind and glowing stranger, a ray of sunshine in the darkness of war, whose name was Ariel, and who pens this letter.*"

Just then, two Gestapo agents came walking down the street. Hanz stood frozen. Three hours of torture was enough for anyone. "Don't be afraid," said Ariel, noting the fear in Hanz' eyes. The Nazis enjoyed the fear they instilled in the people. If you looked afraid, you would most likely be stopped and asked for identification. The agents walked right past him without giving him a second glance, as if he were not there.

He turned to the stranger who had been standing next to him but was startled to find he had vanished without a sound. Hanz stood speechless for a few moments, then he ran the last two blocks to his apartment building. He quickly retired and slept more soundly than he had in over a month.

A week later, Hanz went to see his friend, Brother James, a Benedictine Monk, at the nearby St. Boniface Abbey in Munich. Hanz had met Brother James some months before, and they became close friends. After Hanz would be stopped by Gestapo agents for random questioning, he would visit the Abbey. An hour spent with Brother James in the sanctuary more than compensated for any abuse he may have endured beforehand. Tonight was no different.

The door creaked as it opened. The faint sounds of Brother James and several other monks chanting ancient Gregorian chants in the sanctuary echoed through the building. It was like walking into another time. Candles flickered, giving a medieval feel to the long, dark hallway leading to the sanctuary. Hanz made his way to the sanctuary. The singing had stopped and the monks were chatting as Hanz entered..

"Hanz," Brother James greeted him. "Are you all right? You look terrible."

"I don't want to talk about it right now, Brother."

The monk nodded and said, "Of course. Will you join us for a chant or two? We're just practicing tonight. As Dietrich Bonhoeffer has said, Music will help dissolve your perplexities and purify your character and sensibilities, and in time of care and sorrow, will keep a fountain of joy in you."

"I would love to join you, Brother, " agreed Hanz.

One of the monks passed Hanz a copy of the Greek text of Kyrie Eleison and they were soon chanting.

"Kyrie Eleison, Kyrie Eleison, Christe Eleison, Christe Eleison." (Lord, have mercy, Lord, have mercy, Christ, have mercy, Christ, have mercy)

The choir master would sing first, then the others would repeat it in beautiful unison. The ancient tones, echoing off the ornate wooden Gothic style choir stalls which surrounded them, were very beautiful. After singing an hour or so, Brother James raised his hands toward heaven and knelt to pray. The other monks and Hanz followed his example. Hanz left refreshed by this act of simple yet devout worship of God. It was a practice that brought him much comfort..

Brother James, who shared Hanz's anti-Nazi sentiments, often told him during his visits to the sanctuary, "Brother Hanz, the more physical or emotional abuses abound, the greater the comfort of Christ abounds in you." It was certainly true in Hanz's case.

Chapter 3

A MEETING AT DACHAU

It was a chilly day in October. The wind blew hard in the faces of the SS soldiers on guard at the front and sides of the train which transported prisoners either to their deaths or to other camps down the tracks toward Southern Germany. This train, one of several lines of the *Deutsche Reichsbahn,* was headed for the northeast part of a town called Dachau.

The Nazis built Dachau, a concentration camp, on the grounds of an abandoned munitions factory. It was originally made for political prisoners in 1937, but now held a wide range of prisoners, all of whom had one common goal: survival. They were in constant fear of being selected for random torture such as standing in tiny cells in which the prisoner could not move left or right without being pierced by nails which had been driven through the walls. They had to remain perfectly still until an officer came to release them. Random floggings of unsuspecting prisoners kept the fear strong, and the escape attempts low.

One of the passengers on the train was Sophia Reinstein. She was both happy and fearful of the sudden transfer to Southern Germany. She would be only about twenty miles from where Agnes lived, so she might be able to get a letter to her occasionally. By the same token, she had heard many graphic stories from those who had come from Dachau. Her hands trembled as the train began to slow down, about half a mile from the entrance to the camp.

Soon the train came to a stop. The steam blasted out from under the train as the brake was pulled. Then came the chaos. SS officers with German Shepherds and Kapos with whips and sticks herded the many passengers, beating them as they went. Dogs were barking and people screaming.

A middle-aged man approached Sophia. He was tall, mostly bald, and wore glasses. "Here, let me help you down, child," he said kindly. Sophia accepted thankfully. He was slender but none the less strong. "I am Martin Niemoller."

"Sophia Reinstein."

"Pleasure to meet you."

"How long have you been here?"

Niemoller replied, "Not so long. I was a minister in Berlin and spoke against the Nazification of the Church. It didn't take the Nazis long to get me out of the picture. I have been in and out of several camps over the years. Come, you must get into line. They are going to ask for people with particular skills. You must choose one."

"Why?" asked Sophia.

"Just trust me. I will meet with you later this evening in the yard," Niemoller said.

"SILENCE!" came an authoritative voice over the loudspeaker. "You have arrived at Dachau. You are in Southern Germany. This is a labor camp. You will work hard and be fed. Unfortunately, typhus has been reported in several labor camps around Eastern Poland, so in order to keep things sanitary, you will each have a shower. Naturally, men and women will shower separately. Your clothes will be washed and disinfected. This is just a precaution. We welcome you."

As the line moved slowly forward, the officers would shout, "We need experienced seamstresses, tailors, shoemakers!"

A voice here and there would say, "Here sir! I am a shoemaker" or "I am a tailor." or "I am a seamstress." One of several officers would respond by checking them over, asking them where they had worked and then, if satisfied, would say, "All right, step forward."

"Here, sir! I am a seamstress." called Sophia.

An officer came over and asked her where she had worked.

"Treblinka, for a couple weeks, and before that I made clothes for homeless children in Munich."

He had a kinder face than the others. He reached forward and pulled her gently out of the crowd. "Step forward." He smiled a bit as he turned away.

For some reason, this left an impression on her. *"Why was he gentle and not rough like the other guards? He was intimidating of course, as were all the others with the green uniforms and gun belt. But there was something different about him."*

The gates to her left were opened, and those prisoners who did not have skills were led off to the showers down a long and mostly hidden path. A few minutes later came faint, hellish screams from a building amidst the trees. Then black smoke belched from a solitary chimney that rose ominously high above the trees. Sophia was grieved to know those innocent people had been put to death.

Those who had been picked for work were taken to a separate shower facility. The hot shower was refreshing after the long, stressful train ride. Then they were taken to the sorting sheds for a clean set of clothes and other items they might find useful.

Sophia was taken to the end of a muddy lane lined with rows of buildings that served as the prisoner sleeping barracks and the workshops.. The women in her barracks were friendly to her, treating her like family. This was a common thing in the camps. Total strangers pulling together and forming friendships. She and the other women were taken to the seamstress shop to start work.

After work that evening, Sophia was in the recreation yard playing chess with her new friend Maria. The kind man who had introduced himself as Martin Niemoller approached her. He smiled and said, "I see you took my advice and called out your skill. Good. We save as many as we can." Sophia thanked him.

The weeks passed, and more trainloads of people arrived, but few among them were selected for labor.

One afternoon after work, Sophia made her way to where Martin Niemoller and several priests were talking quietly, periodically kneeling for prayer. It looked like something she would enjoy too. She quietly approached during one of their prayers. A priest was praying, "And so our Father, in thy mercy, let us continue to minister to those our captors. In the name of our Saviour, Jesus Christ. Amen."

Martin Niemoller looked up to see her kneeling with them. "Have we an angel in our midst?" and the others laughed. "Welcome Sophia."

After chatting for a few minutes, Sophia asked, "Pastor Niemoller, can you get a letter out for me?"

Niemoller hesitated. "Oh, I don't know Sophia. The SS screen every letter or postcard that leaves the camp. I fear that would be very dangerous for you. If it had anything to do with the true nature of this camp, they would kill you. The Nazis are monsters. Sergeant Reinhardt is the worst. He's the man in charge of the prisoners here."

"I understand," said Sophia.

Then one of the priests noticed a small boy lurking in the trees on the outside of the camp. The priest pointed the boy out to Niemoller. A knowing look passed between them. Maybe there was a way to get a message out.

"All right, Sophia," said Niemoller. "We will try. Write out a short letter and meet me here tomorrow after work." He handed her a small piece of paper. "Go to your own quarters. Be careful my child."

The next day felt like an eternity. Every passing hour, the rattle of the sewing machine grew more and more monotonous.. About four o'clock that afternoon, Sophia returned to the corner of the recreation yard where her friend, Niemoller again sat with the other priests discussing deep theological topics, such as Greek and Hebrew references. She shyly approached them.

"Don't be shy, Sophia. Come over here," Niemoller said, beckoning with his hand. "Do you have the letter?"

"Yes. I do. Right here."

He put his hand on hers and quietly exclaimed, "No. Secretly. Put it in this Bible I found in the sorting shed." He handed her the Bible, opened to a passage in the New Testament.

She read a little of the passage and carefully slipped the folded letter onto the page. Her hands shook as she realized she had nearly made a deadly mistake.

He quickly closed the Bible and walked over to a bench near the fence. He opened it again and began to write notes in the unused spaces of Sophia's letter. After about five minutes, he folded it and reached his hand behind his back. He smiled when the feeling of little hands met his large, boney ones. The little boy they had seen the night before had agreed to smuggle the letter out of the camp and to Agnes in nearby Munich.

The little boy, whose name was Micah, tore off toward Munich on his bicycle. It took him about an hour to get there at full speed. As he neared Mandelstrasse, he saw two policemen standing on the corner laughing, being quite drunk. Micah was fearful but continued to peddle toward them. He was going at a pretty good clip, but it felt like he was peddling against a strong wind.

Micah saw a man dressed in white at the light pole. The man raised his hands in the direction of the policemen, and they were suddenly gripped with panic. "Something is wrong. Everything is spinning!" one of the policemen exclaimed. The man in white beckoned to frightened Micah. In a moment, the boy was at the corner of

Mendelstrasse. He passed the policemen slumped on the park bench in a deep sleep. He looked up to speak to the stranger in white who had been standing there, but now the stranger was standing at the entrance to Agnes's apartment house, a hundred feet from the corner where the man had been just seconds before. This was as frightening as seeing the drunken policemen. *"How could the man in white have gotten from the corner to the apartment house that quickly?"*

Micah peddled over and put his bike up against the railing. The stranger was standing on the steps. He smiled as Micah cautiously walked past him. No sooner had Micah put his hand on the doorknob and looked back, the man in white had vanished. Micah stood there stunned for a second, then ran up the three flights of stairs.. He rapped on the door and it soon opened a crack.

"Who is it?" Hanz asked gruffly.

"It is Micah," he whispered. He looked at the name on the letter and said, "I have a letter for Agnes Weiss."

Hanz quickly opened the door and pulled the boy inside, then put the deadbolt lock into place.

Agnes joined them when she heard her name. "Who sent you here?" she asked.

"A minister named Niemoller. He told me it was a letter from someone named Sophia. He gave me a gold ring for taking it to you." He produced a small ring with Jewish symbols on the outside.

"Where did the minister get this?" asked Hanz.

"From the sorting shed, I think," said Micah.

Micah wanted to leave, so Hans led him to the door. "Thank you for the letter. It is from a friend of my sister."

The boy smiled and walked quietly down the stairs. Hanz heard the front door below close moments later.

Agnes opened the letter and read it aloud. It said that Dachau was not a death camp like Treblinka, but many still died every day from sickness or abuse. Sophia told of her meeting Pastor Niemoller being a blessing, as she would have someone to talk to after long days in the seamstress shop. "I will be fine here, Agnes," she wrote. "Do not worry about me."

Agnes, in tears, put the letter down on the coffee table and walked over to the window. "Sophia is going to be fine, Agnes," said Hanz. "Now go check on Aaron."

Agnes dried her eyes and went to the storage space where Aaron, the little Jewish orphan, sat cowering in the corner behind some coats. "Come," she assured him. "It's all right. A letter from a friend was delivered. You need not be afraid."

Chapter 4

THE ROAD TO HEAVEN

Through the night, Sophia could hear the screams of selected prisoners undergoing forced and brutal medical experiments performed by sadistic SS doctors, such as Dr. Klaus Schilling and Dr. Sigmund Rascher. One experiment plunged the naked victims into a tank of freezing water. Dissenting Polish priests were among the victims of these experiments. She worried about her friend Pastor Niemoller.

After about three weeks at Dachau, rumors of a new shipment of seven hundred Jews and political prisoners made their way around the camp. "When are they supposed to be coming?" asked a man.

"Tomorrow, maybe the day after," answered another. "I don't know, but soon. They are liquidating a ghetto and they need room here. We will probably be transferred elsewhere before then."

The next day, during mealtime, the haunting name of Auschwitz-Birkenau trickled through the camp as their destination in the event of a transfer. One of Sophia's

Jewish friends, Karl, was sitting next to her when the news came. His face grew ashen. The filthy pan of watery soup spilled onto his feet. "O mein Gott! Dies ist das ende!" ("Oh my God! This is the end!") he said, rubbing his forehead nervously.

"Where are we going?" Sophia asked, taking another gulp of her soup.

"Auschwitz," replied Karl.

Her hands went numb at the answer. "Au-auschwitz?" she stuttered. "Are you sure about that?"

"Yes. Are you religious?" asked Karl.

"Yes. I- I guess," answered Sophia.

"Then it would be smart to prepare yourself, Sophia. If you end up on the train, you will die," said Karl.

"All right, back to work!" came the angry voice of the Oberkapo. The crowd quickly dispersed, each one returning to their separate workshops.

Sophia tried to block the terror from her mind by immersing herself in her work. It seemed to be working until the black train pulled into the yard.

An hour later, seven hundred prisoners, including Sophia, were herded into the train cars, and the doors were locked. A blast of steam pierced the air and the train was soon racing down the tracks toward southern Poland.

Sophia was not prepared for what might be the final stage of her life. The entire trip, she was overcome by the fear of the unknown and the certain death that lay waiting only a few hours ahead. She trembled and sobbed the last half hour of the journey.

A few miles from the town of Auschwitz, the stench of the crematorium met her nostrils. Soon the camp gate came into view, with its brick construction and observation tower that stood over the center of the tracks. She dropped to her knees and committed her soul to God and asked Him to send His angels to take her home to heaven.

Sophia's tears fell as the doors were opened and hundreds of people jumped from the train. Those too old or too weak to jump were carried to a rough wooden cart. The rest were separated into two groups, men and women. An officer gave a brief and rehearsed speech about his fear that typhus might break out in the camp. They would all be given a hot shower while their clothes were disinfected. The two groups were quickly ushered off through different gates. A sign hung above the gate through which Sophia's group went that read: "*Weg zum Himmel*" *(*"Road to Heaven") For Sophia, it would certainly be the road to heaven.

The Nazis used the shower facilities because it held many people. They knew many would welcome a hot shower after the stressful train trip and walk right into the trap. The Zyklon B gas they used at Auschwitz would not work when mixed with water, so the Nazis did not waste any time getting the gas crystals down the overhead hatch.

Sophia and the other women and children waited in the shower area for the hot water to be turned on, but nothing happened. Everyone stood there dumbfounded, looking at each other with frightened expressions on their faces and whispering. The hatch opened above them, and a hail of light blue crystals rained down onto the dusty floor and turned into a poisonous gas.

What happened next was something Sophia thought was hell on earth. Hundreds of naked and helpless human beings screaming and clawing at the cement walls, gasping desperately for air.

Panic gripped Sophia when she was hit with a cloud of the gas. She tried in vain to utter a scream as her airway rapidly swelled and she could not breath. Her body shook violently and she raised her hands toward heaven to commit her spirit to God.

Suddenly everything went numb and silent, and she collapsed along with the others. The screaming had stopped. The untold pain she had just experienced was also gone. A strong and pleasant voice called to her. It was the same guard who had been kind to her at Dachau. Only now, he wore an overcoat, pin-striped trousers, and patent leather shoes. He smiled and said, "Remember me?"

She returned a smile and said, "Of-of course I remember you. You were the guard who took me out for work detail at Dachau."

"Yes. Except I am not an SS guard." His clothes began to glow polished gold. "God heard your prayer this morning on the train, when you asked for angels to take you home. I am an angel of those who pass over to God into their heavenly home."

Sophia watched as the entire room was flooded with light, like a beautiful sunrise. The scene changed from a filthy building to a view of the Heavenly City. Sophia was suddenly clothed in white. The gates of pearl, emerald and walls of jasper were glorious. The gates opened, and the first thing she saw were outstretched hands marred by jagged nail scars. The Saviour was there to welcome her home.

Thus was the Home-going of Sophia Reinstein.

Chapter 5

THE VISITORS

The parade and rally at Nuremberg was as always, a stunning performance. Hitler and Goebbels gave invigorating patriotic speeches that whipped the huge crowds into a frenzy, chanting the praises of the Third Reich.

After the rally, it was a quarter to midnight when Agnes and Hanz finally made it back to the apartment. Agnes kicked off her heels and threw herself onto the sofa and said, "I need to do some dusting for a few minutes. I'm wound up like a watch spring."

Hanz laughed and said, "You know, it's kind of rewarding defying the Nazis orders about helping Jews.

"I know what you mean. But it's still scary every time I bring food to the Heislers or when I buy extra food at the market for Aaron. The clerk gives me a strange look whenever I go in there now."

Hanz retired to his room to read while Agnes dusted. She had just moved a vase from the coffee table in order to dust beneath it when there was a knock on the door. This sound had become an object of mortal fear since the occupation of Munich. The vase slipped from her hands, shattering on the floor. She gasped as she made her way to the door. Her heart pounded. The lower part of her body felt numb and heavily weighed down. She opened the door a crack.

A young lad about ten years old dressed in rags stood at the door. Tears streaked down his face. "Please, my father is sick, and he needs bread."

Agnes, being a compassionate creature, said, "Come in. You should not be out this time of night. Someone might see you here." She closed the door to remove the chain lock. When she opened the door again, the little boy was running down the stairs. Before her stood two fully uniformed SS officers in heavy gray coats. Agnes gasped and put her trembling hand to her mouth.

The first officer pushed her aside and was now standing in her living room. The other stood silently in the doorway.

"Wh-what's going on here?" cried Agnes.

"You are hiding and giving aid to the Jews. That automatically incurs you the death penalty. Were you not aware of this law?" asked the officer.

"I- well of course, but I don't give aid," said Agnes.

"Now, now!" he scolded, holding a finger up to his lips. "You know, I really hate it when people lie to me! You have been helping the Heisler family across the street, and we have information that you are keeping a young Jewish lad here. Are you still going to deny this?"

"The Heisler's are my friends. What was I supposed to do?" cried Agnes.

"Obey the Reich laws! Tell me," he asked, noticing the Bible on the shelf, "What does it say in that book about following the laws of the government that God has set over you, hmm?"

"There comes a time, sir, when we must make decisions that shape who we are. I chose to obey the laws of God instead of the Reich. Sir, it also says in that Book in Romans 10:12: "For there is no difference between the Jew and the Greek: for the same Lord over all is rich unto all that call upon him. For whosoever shall call upon the name of the Lord shall be saved." The Heislers needed help to get them back on their feet," said Agnes.

The officer chuckled in disbelief and said, "You would risk your own life for someone your own government considers a national security threat?"

By this time, Hanz had heard Agnes talking to someone in the living room. With his bedroom door open a crack, he could see what was happening. He quietly crept over to his closet and began packing his prison bag with some wool stockings, heavy sweaters and a couple pairs of warm trousers.

"Fraulein, we have orders to take you and your brother Hanz to Eastern Poland. You have five minutes to pack some warm clothes and come with us. Get moving."

Agnes' heart was pounding as she hurried into the bedroom and found that Hanz was already packed. "This is not happening," Agnes said.

"Yes, it is, Agnes. We knew the risks when we decided to break the law."

Five minutes later, the officers escorted them down the three flights of stairs. They passed a Gestapo agent. "You got to them first, huh?" said the agent.

"You were too slow," said the SS officer. The Gestapo agent shook his head and left. A black government car was waiting for them at the curb. The other officer opened the rear door and said in a low, haunting voice, "Get in."

What happened next was something that neither Agnes nor Hanz could explain. When the officer began to drive away from the curb, a brief and strange feeling came over them. It was the same kind of feeling you get sledding fast down a slippery slope. The force pushed them back in their seats.

Suddenly the Polish border checkpoint came into view. Hanz looked at his sister in disbelief. It was nearly a twelve-hour trip by car, and they had only just started moving a minute or two before. The car drove right through the gate, which opened itself as they pulled up to it, and they continued driving for about twenty minutes. A narrow pathway appeared on the left, which disappeared into the dark spruce forest.

The officer driving turned and said, "This is where you get out. The ride's over."

Hanz was confused. "I don't understand. I thought you were SS officers."

The driver said with a smile, "You never want to make assumptions, Hanz." His voice seemed to change, and now had a slight echo, like he was far away. The two officers looked at each other and nodded. The entire interior of the car lit up like a golden sunrise, getting brighter every moment. "We are not SS officers. We are sent to take you out of the battle. You did well."

"Angels," breathed Agnes.

"Straight from God. There are angels in the Third Reich, Agnes. You've got nothing to be afraid of now." He turned and put his hand on Hanz's shoulder. "Especially you, Hanz."

Until now, Hanz's tricep had been giving him much pain from his torture. The angel touched the bruised flesh, and the pain left. The other angel took out a map of the surrounding area and said, "Read this map carefully. These little marks here are locations you want to stay away from. That's where the SS will be patrolling tonight. Now once you get past them, keep walking until you find the Partisans. Actually, they will find you. They, too, patrol the forests. You'll be safe with them for the time being."

Thank you very much," said Agnes, "but you really gave us quite a scare."

"Well, we had to observe your reaction to the ultimate test - the possible loss of life. You did very well. Now go. You don't have any time to waste."

Hanz and his sister stepped out of the car and it vanished almost as soon as it started moving. They knelt on the damp ground and offered a prayer of thanks for the experiences they would remember for the rest of their lives. But there was one final test for them before they left.

A Nazi patrol jeep came racing up the road and stopped a few hundred feet before them and shined the bright spotlight around. When it came to rest on them, Hanz and Agnes froze.

"It's a couple of deer, you idiot!," exclaimed one of the officers. "Come on. Let's get back to the post!". They sped off in the other direction.

Thus was the final act of supernatural protection Hanz and Agnes experienced for the remainder of the war. They found the Partisan's camp and eventually escaped out of Nazi occupied territory. Aaron, the boy they cared for, was picked up by a local contact of the Partisans and taken in as one of their own.

Hanz opened a ski shop in Switzerland near the *Andermatt* ski resort. Agnes moved to Geneva after the war. Her children never get tired of the stories she recounts to them about the Angels of the Third Reich.

"Being a Christian is less about cautiously avoiding sin than about courageously and actively doing God's will." Dietrich Bonhoeffer – German pastor and Nazi dissident, executed by the Nazis in 1945.

Das Ende

ANGELS OF THE THIRD REICH: SONGS IN THE NIGHT

BOOK TWO

Luebben,
Nazi Occupied Germany
April, 1943

"The golden sunbeams with their joyous gleams,
Are kindling for earth, her life and mirth,
Shedding forth lovely and heart cheering light.
Through the dark hours chill I lay silent and still,
But risen at length to gladness and strength,
I gaze on the heavens all glowing and bright."

Paul Gerhardt, 17th Century

Chapter 1

A STORM APPROACHES

The second world war had been raging in Europe since early September of 1939, when Germany attacked Poland. Germany was in economic collapse. With Adolf Hitler's powerful speeches and promises of economic reform, he became a messiah to the German populous when he first came to power between the years of 1931-1933. However, he soon became an unthinkable nightmare.

In the village of Luebben, the Kohler house is surrounded by a neatly kept lawn. In back of the house, there is a garden in which tender new sprouts of early vegetables and herbs grow in perfectly straight rows.

Elizabeth Kohler, twenty years old, who had been a student of Musical History at the prestigious Berlin University of the Arts in Charlottenburg, leaned out over the porch railing watching her father gardening. Aside from spending time with his children, Richard Kohler loved gardening the most. He loved getting his hands in the cool, black soil of the garden and providing tender care for the plants. Elizabeth smiled to see him so happy with such simplicity.

When Elizabeth was twelve, her mother passed away from dropsy (congestive heart failure.) Toward the end of her life, she developed severe pulmonary edema. Her lungs filled with fluid so that she struggled to get a breath. Tears of fear and pain streamed down her face as she aspirated a bloody fluid, gasping in vain for a breath of air. The image of such suffering was something Elizabeth would never fully get over. Afterward, however, the rest of the family became closer than they ever had been.

Elizabeth's older brother, Richie, was in the regular army and did not work directly for the Nazis. The Nazis comprise of the Gestapo; SA (Sturmabteilung), Storm Detachment/Assault Division or Brownshirts as they were known, and the SS (Schutzstaffel), an elite organization within the Nazi party that served as Hitler's personal guard. The SS included police units and special forces carrying out mass killings of civilians and overseeing concentration camps.

Richie was well aware of the cruelty Jews all over Europe were experiencing. Being a moral young man, Richie opposed respect shown only to those of a certain race. He believed that Jews or any people are of the same blood as he and that they should be treated as such, not being beaten or having racial slander painted on the windows of their shops.

Richie wrote in a journal his thoughts on the matter:

"It hurts me much to see my countrymen lost in a dark sea of needless hatred and clouded minds toward those who are of a different race. Throughout Germany, especially Berlin, the random abuse of the Jewish people cannot be justified. Homeless Jewish children, many of whom are no more than twelve years of age, huddle in the alleys at night, trying to keep warm. Nearly all pass by without offering a second glance, let alone help. All who are caught helping Jews are shot, except for a few SS officers who may show mercy to first time offenders, giving them strong warning. I am reminded of the Bible verse Galatians 6:10: "*As we have therefore opportunity, let us do good unto all men, especially unto them who are of the household of faith.*" Perhaps I can help somehow."

Earlier this year, Richie was on the eastern front, in a tiny village. He had been given his orders. Now perched in the bell tower of the church, all he had to do was wait with his Mauser 8mm K98k rifle. He was a sniper and a valued asset to his company. At 2:30 that afternoon, he saw an infantry battalion approaching from the south. His hands were shaking now, something he had grown accustomed to before a battle. He gave the signal, and the men took their positions throughout the little village.

The battle soon began and lasted for the next four hours. Being a sniper required him to kill the enemy. Richie was a merciful man, and always aimed for the vital areas, head, neck or heart, for an instantaneous and painless kill. At these times he would quote a Bible verse to himself. It seemed to help with concentration. *"Blessed be the Lord, my strength, which teacheth my hands to war, and my fingers to fight: my goodness and my fortress, my high tower and my deliverer, my shield, and he in whom I trust." (Psalm 144:1-2)*

At one point during this battle, Richie was adjusting his scope and sighting in another enemy when a mortar exploded in mid-air about ten feet from the bell tower. Richie was blown out of the tower. A jagged piece of shrapnel, which nearly went through his thigh, protruded out of the back of his leg.

As he lay dazed and writhing in pain on the muddy ground, an old, white-haired man approached him. Richie thought the old man did not fit into the scene in any way. His clothes were not wet, even though it was raining. He wore a suit, brown leather shoes, and a dark overcoat. He stooped next to Richie and cared for him, binding up the massive wound with a piece of clean cloth. The bleeding slowed, and the old man spoke words of comfort that brought great peace to Richie in this traumatic event.

"Are they not all ministering spirits, sent forth to minister for them who shall be heirs of salvation?" (Hebrews 1:14)

Richie distinctly remembers that the man's spotless Homburg hat and the shoulders of his coat faintly glowed of deep gold. When the man touched him, the pain left until he awoke in the field hospital. A chaplain at the hospital told Richie that Jesus himself taught that everyone who puts their trust in Him has their own angel to guard them and give them help in times of adversity.

The chaplain continued, "When Moses came down out of the mountains, after being only a little while in the presence of God, his face glowed. The fact that you could see the visible glow was the effect of living in the perpetual light of God's presence. It shouldn't surprise you Richie that the old man who helped you had a glow about his entire body."

"Take heed that ye despise not one of these little ones; for I say unto you. That in heaven their angels do always behold the face of my Father which is in heaven."(Matthew 18:10)

After Ritchie's release from the hospital, he was given a medal of honor and discharged from the army. He slowly regained his strength and set a goal for himself: to be able to walk to the seventeenth century church about a quarter mile from the house.

It took Richie two weeks to be able to hobble to the church. When he did, he offered a prayer of thanks to God. It became a habit every evening for Richie to walk to the church for prayer, and it was there that he found his love for singing.

It was Sunday evening about eight-thirty. The moon rose slowly above the trees, turning from a reddish gold to a bright white by the time it had fully risen. Richie had just made it to the steps of the church when the door opened. A stout man who appeared to be in his late sixties held open the door and welcomed him inside. He wore the typical clerical robes and a rather outdated collar that appeared to have been from the seventeenth century. He had an irresistible charm that caused Richie to smile.

"Welcome." He greeted Richie. "Do you live far?"

"Only a quarter mile or so. I was injured in the war, so this seemed like a good destination to try to get back on my feet."

"Yes indeed." He smiled and extended his hand. "I'm Paul."

Richie shook his hand. "I'm Richie. Nice to meet you, though I didn't expect to meet anyone here at this hour."

"This place inspired me to write many years ago."

"What do you write?"

"Poems mostly. Like this one. He handed Richie a piece of fine paper. On it was written several verses done in the classic Gothic font. "Read this, son," Paul said with a warm smile.

The words were simple and beautiful.

"The golden sunbeams with their joyous gleams,

Are kindling o'er earth, her life and mirth,
Shedding forth lovely and heart-cheering light,
Through the dark hours' chill I lay silent and still,
But risen at length to gladness and strength,
I gaze on the heavens all glowing and bright.

Mine eyes now behold thy works, that of old and ever
Are telling to all men here dwelling.
How great is thy glory, how wondrous thy power;
They tell of the home where the faithful shall come,
Who depart to the peace that can change not or cease,
From earth where all passeth as passes the hour."

The words captivated Richie. He thought this had to be a very special old man to be able to write in such a way. Paul prayed with him, and Richie left for home. It was late, and the walk had tired him. He read the script on the way home in the bright moonlight, and suddenly a tune came to him and he began to sing the words. The words were written in such a way that you would automatically begin to sing them.

He was still singing the words as he walked into the kitchen where Elizabeth was washing dishes. "Where did you learn that?" she asked him, drying her hands.

"An old man at the church said he wrote it. Here's a copy."

She opened it and read the handwritten document. "That's one of Paul Gerhardt's lesser known hymns. You said there is an old man at the church?"

"Yes. Why?"

"Because that's the Paul Gerhardt church. It is where Paul Gerhardt was archdeacon and preached from 1669 to 1676. What was the old man like?"

"He was in his late sixties, quite stocky and had a mustache. Oh, and he wore a priest's robe."

"Did he give you his name?"

"His name is Paul. Why all the questions?"

Elizabeth did not know how to answer, so remained silent for the time, uttering a quiet, "Hmm." *How could this be possible? A renowned hymn writer who died centuries ago returned to his beloved church to help an ailing young man who had put his whole trust in God. This was impossible,* Elizabeth thought. *Yet even Jesus' disciples believed that ghosts could appear before men. Perhaps it really wasn't all that impossible after all. Time will tell.*

About midnight, Richie was awakened by a rap on the door. He took with him to the door the K-98k rifle, which he had kept from the war. Hello?" he said cautiously, cracking the door slightly.

"H-help me!" said the weak voice of an old man, wheezing as he spoke. Richie thought he was a starving old German man, collateral damage of the war and helped him inside. Then he saw the faded yellow armband and the Jewish star. Richie's heart began to pound.

Richie's hatred of the Nazis continued to deepen. He had killed before, and if the Gestapo came for him, he thought he could do it again.

Elizabeth, aroused by the noise downstairs, came to see what was going on. She was startled to see Richie talking to the old man in the living room. "Oh Richie. What have you done?!"

"What was I supposed to do, Elizabeth, leave this man starving at my door?"

"You know the Reich's laws. We could all die because of this."

Richie recited the words of Jesus. *"Inasmuch as ye have done it unto one of the least of these my brethren, ye have done it unto me."* (Matthew 25:40)

Elizabeth sighed and said, "Alright, we'll do it your way."

"What on earth is going on down there!" came their father's voice from his bedroom. Herr Kohler walked out and braced himself on the door frame. "What is this?"

"Shalom, Herr Kohler," said the old man with a pleasant and deep voice. He smiled whilst sipping a cup of tea Elizabeth had made for him. "I am Adam Engel."

"Shalom. Welcome." Kohler's intent was to ask the man to leave, but his words could only come as a blessing and a welcome to his mysterious guest.

"I called thee to curse mine enemies, and behold, thou hast altogether blessed them . . . " (Numbers.24:10)

Richie and Elizabeth helped Adam Engel get settled in the spare bedroom upstairs. Although fear accompanied hiding the old man, with it came the satisfaction of doing the will of God.

That night a heaviness was felt by the Kohler siblings, like when a storm approaches. An ominous black cloud looms, silhouetting the trees. The feeling becomes stronger as it comes ever closer. It was the feeling of impending doom.

There was a storm brewing in Berlin that involved the father of Richie and Elizabeth. Herr Kohler had been involved in politics in Berlin when Hitler was running for office in the early 1930's. He had stepped on the wrong toes and now it was time to settle the score. He had been labeled a threat by the National Security Office and through various informants, the Gestapo was ready to make an arrest.

Chapter 2

THE ARRESTS

Richie continued to walk to the church each evening to pray, and his friend Paul continued to teach him the hymns he had written and soon began to teach Richie the parts of harmony.

Elizabeth would hear Richie return home singing the hymns. She now knew it must somehow be Paul Gerhardt. She went with Richie to the church the next evening but waited outside the sanctuary.

She heard a voice say, "Good evening, Richie. Have you been able to get any practice?"

"Yes, I have. Actually I practice whilst working in the garden."

"Splendid! Um, what is your sister's name?"

"Elizabeth. How did you know I had a sister?"

"Why is she hiding outside the door? Please, tell her to come in!"

The door creaked, and Elizabeth timidly walked down the aisle. Paul extended his hand. His hands were warm and strong, as was his whole appearance.

That night, Elizabeth and Richie learned to harmonize together, something they had never done. They sang some beautiful verses, such as those of *"Wie Soll Ich Dich Empfangen."* or *"Lord, How Shall I Meet Thee?"*

"O Lord how shall I meet Thee, how welcome Thee aright?
Thy people long to greet Thee, my Hope, my heart's Delight!
O kindle, Lord, most holy, Thy lamp within my breast
To do in spirit lowly all that may please Thee best.

Thy Zion strews before Thee green boughs and fairest palms;
And I, too, will adore Thee with joyous songs and psalms.
My heart shall bloom forever for Thee with praises new
And from Thy name shall never withhold the honor due."

Verse after verse, Elizabeth and Richie sang together, quickly gaining confidence and volume. The sweet voices caused the occasional passerby to turn aside to listen. Even a dangerous and political SS officer or local policeman would stop from his beat to listen. The songs in the night drew them in for a few moments of respite from the stress of the times. When it was over, they put their hats back on and resumed their duties.

"Music will dissolve your perplexities, and purify your character and sensibilities, and in time of care and sorrow, will keep a fountain of joy in you." (Dietrich Bonhoeffer, anti-Nazi dissident, was arrested in 1943 by the Gestapo accused of being assossiated with the plot to assassinate Adolf Hitler. He was hanged on April 9, 1945.)

Perhaps it was the fountain of joy that continued to spring up in Richie and Elizabeth's lives that kept them going in the days ahead. For those days would indeed bring much sorry and pain for them both.

A chill lingered in the air one night. Richie was having trouble sleeping. The post-traumatic stress was kicking in. When he fell asleep, it would be restless and filled with graphic dreams of the war. Images of the people he had killed as a sniper refused to leave him alone. Their screams for mother or a lover rang loud in his ears. He would often awake in a cold sweat, holding his head. Tonight was no different.

Elizabeth was also awake and heard her brother tossing in his bed. She prayed that night for her brother. Tears of sibling sympathy filled her eyes as she prayed for God to touch him.

Richie got up to get a sleeping powder. But before taking it, he was struck with a heavy feeling of sleep. He had just enough time to get back into bed before falling into a deep peaceful sleep until seven-thirty the next morning. He made his way down the stairs to the kitchen, rubbing his eyes. He was not quite out of the blissful borders of repose, but the land of the real world would soon become the victor.

"Morning, sleepy head," Elizabeth greeted.

Richie said, "I haven't slept that well in years. I barely had enough time to get back into bed. I feel wonderful though."

"It must have been your angel, you know, the one who helped you when you were alone on that bloody ground." *Elizabeth could not believe her prayer for her brother had been answered so quickly.*

"Oh, yea. How can I forget that?" Richie said.

The old Jew, Adam Engel, came downstairs presently and joined the rest of the family. The breakfast consisted of fresh vegetables lightly cooked in a light cream sauce.

Dairy products were rationed during the war. The stamps issued for foodstuffs, such as bread, allowed for only about half a loaf, and 1200 grams of meat (about 2.5 pounds per day or less.) As meat was also becoming hard to find, some families in the rural areas raised rabbits and chickens. Many families had a small garden where they harvested herbs and garlic which would have been expensive in the local market. They also grew different root and leaf crops like carrots, beets, spinach. Herr Kohler surely had a green thumb. Whatever he set his mind to raise in their little backyard garden would grow very well.

Engel sat down at the table and put his napkin in his lap. Before eating, he raised his hands and offered a beautiful Hebrew blessing over the food. "*In God we boast all the day long, and praise thy name for ever, Selah.*" (Psalm 44:8) He took a mouthful of his breakfast and began smiling. "What did you put in this, Elizabeth?"

"Fresh vegetables from the garden, Herr Engel. The sauce was just condensed milk and a little cheese."

"It's very satisfying food, young lady. I think I'm going to enjoy my stay here."

As Richie sat intently observing their guest, a verse came to him. The words of Matthew 25:35 resonated through his mind. *"I was an hungered and ye gave me meat. I was thirsty, and ye gave me drink. I was a stranger, and ye took me in."* The words worked on Richie, who was still uncomfortable in sheltering a Jew. Eventually, he accepted the lot he had been given.

As Richie and Elizabeth prepared again to go to the church to be taught by their friend Paul, Elizabeth's friend from the university, Sarah Hess and her friend, David Leider, stopped in. They asked that they be allowed to come with Elizabeth and Richie to the singing that night.

At the church, Paul came out from behind the curtains that separated the sanctuary from the rest of the church. He looked surprised to see four people sitting there, rather than the two he had been teaching. "What's this, Richie?"

"I'm sorry, Herr Gerhardt, but they insisted on coming." (By now, Gerhardt had confirmed that he was indeed Paul Gerhardt.)

"That is quite alright. Let us begin," Gerhardt said, giving a piece of paper to Richie. He turned to the group and arranged them in a half circle near the ornate choir loft. As if by some supernatural act of blessing, the words came to each of the four in their own part of harmony. The sound was something none of them would ever forget. It was as though they had been singing in a chamber style chorus together for years.

It came as if perfectly natural, even though they had never sung in a group setting before. The words seemed to effect Sarah in particular. She could not help but reflect on the passion of Christ, her Passover they sang the words to *"O Haupt voll Blut und Wunden"* ("O Sacred Head, Now Wounded")

"My Shepherd, now receive me;
My Guardian, own me Thine.
Great blessings Thou didst give me,
O Source of gifts divine!
Thy lips have often fed me
With words of truth and love;
Thy spirit oft hath led me
To heavenly joys above. (Verse 5)

Here I will stand beside Thee,
From Thee I will not part:
O Saviour, do not chide me!
When breaks Thy loving heart,
When soul and body languish
In death's cold, cruel grasp,

Then, in Thy deep anguish,
Thee in my arms I'll clasp." (Verse 6)

Joy filled their hearts, especially when they came to Verse 10 that read:

"Be Thou my Consolation,
My Shield when I must die;
Remind me of Thy passion
When my last hour draws nigh.
Mine eyes shall behold Thee,
Upon Thy cross shall dwell.
My heart by faith enfolds Thee.
Who dieth thus dies well!"

The Passover was now only a couple of days away. Despite the strong and negative political pressure, the Jews were preparing for the celebration. Since Herr Engle showed himself to be a devout Jew, he also prepared for the feast.

On the night of the Passover, Elizabeth was working in the potting shed when the aroma of fresh bread met her nostrils. She set down her pot and went to see what was going on in the kitchen. Herr Engel stood at the oven clad in a striped apron, spotted with flour. He wiped his hands as Elizabeth walked into the kitchen. "What are you doing, Herr Engel?"

"Preparing for the Passover, Elizabeth. There may be a war on, but we should still remember the significance of the event."

"I thought it was forbidden for Jews to celebrate the Passover."

"That may be, but there comes a time, Elizabeth, when you need to make decisions that will make you who you are as an individual. If you were concerned with the current law, you certainly would not have accepted me into your home and fed me. You are aware, are you not, of the law passed stating that all who hide or give aid to the Jews will automatically receive the death penalty?"

"Yes, of course I am aware of it."

"Then why did you decide to help me?"

"Because there is no difference between you and any other man. Jew or not, it makes no difference. All men are created in the image of God."

Engel smiled. "A gracious answer. Now, shall we prepare for the Passover?"

"Yes. Of course." Elizabeth felt a warmth every time she was around Herr Engel. There was just something about him. His calmness was something she learned to enjoy, and found herself coming to him for spiritual advice, since her father was not a religious man.

Before the meal after everyone joined hands. Engel offered a Hebrew blessing on the meal.

Dinner was simple: matzo bread, vegetables in a clear sauce of Engel's making, and canned meat that had to pass as the Paschal Lamb. Conversation was mostly about the war, politics, and Engel touched on the goodness of God. He initiated some of the most interesting conversations ever at the Kohler's dinner table. Even Herr Kohler, who had been mostly quiet around Engel until now, shelled him with all manner of difficult political questions. Herr Engel answered all of them with ease, and to Kohler's satisfaction.

"Herr Engel," he asked, "What is your opinion of our new government, in comparison with the one it replaced?"

"Please, call me Adam, Herr Kohler. What you had between the years of say 1919 and 1933 was a government faced with issues such as hyperinflation, political extremists, from both right and left wing groups, etc. Yet they pulled together and unified tax policies as well as the rail systems for business and transportation, not to mention successfully reforming the currency. The Weimar Republic was, overall, a far better endeavor than the present Reich."

The conversation went on for about two hours.

"Is there nothing you cannot answer, Adam?"

"Well, no. At least not the questions you've been asking, anyway." Adam sighed and rose from the table. "I think I will retire now."

Kohler also rose and shook Adam's hand. "Thank you Adam, for making the conversation lively this evening. It was a pleasure hearing your answers. I must say it has been some time since I've heard that much wisdom and intelligence in a single conversation. I've been out of state politics for too long I suppose."

"Quite possibly, my good man. Good night everyone."

That night Elizabeth and Richie walked to the church as usual, but on the way, Richie noticed a change. The pain from where the shrapnel had hit was gone. In fact, when thinking back on it, it had left when Adam took his hand during the Passover Prayer. "Elizabeth, there's something about Adam. When we joined hands tonight, the pain from my injury left completely. I can't explain that."

"Maybe there's something more to him than meets the eye," said Elizabeth.

"Be not forgetful to entertain strangers: for thereby some have entertained angels unawares." (Hebrews 13:2)

Soon they reached the church. David and Sarah were waiting outside on the steps. David commented that Richie was not limping as he had been the night before. Richie told him it had left that night, though he did not speak of the Jew in his house.

Even though they were friends, David and Sarah could still be working for the Gestapo. That was one of the most difficult parts of being a Christian in Nazi Germany: You wanted to share your feelings for the mistreatment of Jews, and that there was no difference between them and any other man, but therein was the problem. Every block had its informants—children, students, businessmen, and even the elderly. In the Kohler's case, just Richie and his sister were Christian. Their father, Herr Kohler said nothing against this. He also was disgusted with the government's mistreatment of the Jews to gain popularity with the masses.

"Are you ready?" asked David.

"We are indeed. Let's go in," answered Richie.

As usual, Gerhardt handed out copies of his beautiful hymn, "*Warum Sollte Überqueren Und Probe Trauern Mir?*" ("Why Should Cross and Trial Grieve Me?") Gerhardt told them he had written this hymn when he lost four of his five children, as well as his wife.

"*Why should cross and trial grieve me?*
Christ is near, with his cheer;
Never will he leave me.

Who can rob me of the heaven
That God's Son for me won
When his life was given.

God gives me my days of gladness,
And I will trust him still
*When he sends me s*adness.

God is good; His love attends me,
Day by day, come what may,
Guides me and defends me.

Now in Christ, death cannot slay me,
Though it might, day and night,
Trouble and dismay me.

Christ has made my death a portal
From the strife of this life
To his joy immortal."

The quartet fell easily into harmony and sang it to the tune of *"EMBELING"*. When they were finished singing, the friends ended the time in a prayer.

The First Arrest

Later that night, Herr Kohler slept soundly as the wind blew gently through the open window. About one o'clock, he was startled awake by a tall man standing next to his bed wearing an overcoat and hat.

Before he could cry out for help, Kohler was knocked unconscious for a few seconds with the handle of the stranger's revolver. Still dazed, his hands were quickly bound and he was brought outside to a waiting car.
Richie had been awakened by a dream. He went to the window to get a breath of fresh air. He saw two strange men shoving his father into what he knew **was an**

unmarked police car used primarily by the Gestapo. He grabbed his sniper rifle which was leaning against the wall next to him, and reverted back to his sniper mentality. He quoted the verse from Psalms as he had often done.

"Blessed be the Lord, my strength, which teacheth my hands to war, and my fingers to fight: my goodness and my fortress; my high tower and my deliverer, my shield, and he in whom I trust." (Psalm 144:1-2)

He rested the stock on the windowsill and adjusted the scope until the open passenger side window of the car came into view. The moonlight gave him a clear shot. He aimed and squeezed the trigger.

Kohler heard the shot. A bullet entered at the C-2 vertebrae of Officer Hanz Schubert who was sitting in the front passenger seat. It severed both his spinal cord and his carotid artery. He was killed instantly. The shot caused a massive blood spray that hit the windshield as well as the driver.

"Ah! GOD!!!" exclaimed the terrified driver, quickly shielding his face. "Are you alright, Schubert?" The driver still not fully comprehending what had just happened.

But there could be no answer. Blood poured from both Schubert's mouth and the exit wound. His body shook violently for a few seconds, then slumped lifeless into the seat.

"Schubert?!" the driver called, shaking him on the shoulder. When he drew his hand away, it was covered with arterial blood.

A second shot was fired. The 8mm bullet came silently through the rear window about three inches from where Kohler sat, missing the driver's head by inches. Kohler knew his son was good at what he did in the war. He just didn't expect to see its effects so close to him.

The driver panicked. He floored the gas pedal and soon disappeared into the night.

The police car arrived in Berlin at about two-fifteen A.M. at a large brick building on Wilhelmstrasse. Kohler was brought into a small and rather pleasant room. There was only one light on in the room, and that was a small desk lamp directly in front of him.

A handsome middle-aged man in a crisp SS uniform sat behind the ornate walnut desk in an office chair reading a file. He looked over the top of his spectacles and said, "Welcome, Richard Kohler. Please sit down."

Kohler hesitated. "I ahh . . . "

A heavy hand came down unbearably on the top of his shoulder and pushed Kohler into the seat. "The good man said "Sit!" said a voice from behind him.

The interrogating officer smirked and said, "I have been looking over your file, Kohler. It says here that you were once involved in politics in the early thirties, being particularly active when Hitler was running for office. Is that true?"

Kohler nodded. "Yes. I was for several years a supporter of the Centre Party until I was relieved of my office in the Reichstag in February of '30. I wrote a few articles criticizing some of the actions by the government, including the violent attacks on party meetings in Westphalia. I didn't think it was that big of a deal to be honest with you." Kohler shifted uncomfortably in his chair. "There was much political unrest during that time, not to mention rather heated debates amongst all the political parties in the German states."

"And you thought you would add to that unrest?" interrupted his interrogator.

Kohler shook his head vehemently. "No. Not at all. I was an ambitious politician who got caught up in the hottest topics of the day. That's politics. Don't you know what it's like to enjoy what you do?"

"Yes. I do indeed, Kohler. We're keeping you here overnight. You can go in the morning." The officer rose from his chair and walked over to Kohler, motioning him to stand. "I am sorry to have to drag you into this. Tread carefully." He extended his hand, and the unsuspecting Kohler fell into the clutches of a direct threat. The officer bore down on Kohler's hand with his full strength. Kohler could feel the muscles and tendons in his hand burning. "If I ever see you in this room again, you will never return home. Do you understand what I am telling you?" Kohler winced and nodded, and the officer released his grip. "Get him out of here."

Kohler was taken to a small room down the hall where he would spend the night. It had no windows, and the door was bolted from the outside. He sat down on the cot with his head in his hands and thought about his children at home, and what they must be feeling.

As he sat deep in thought, a familiar voice addressed him. He was startled and slipped onto the floor as he tried to stand up. The voice belonged to Adam Engel. "What . . . How did you get in here?" Kohler asked. "The door is locked."

"Locked doors make no difference to us, Kohler," he answered. "Show me your hand. Does it hurt you?" Adam asked.

"It's burning up." Kohler extended his hand, which had now swollen to twice it's normal size.

Adam touched his hand. The pain left, and his hand was restored to its normal size.

Without even asking, Kohler knew that Adam was not a Jew, but an angel. "Who are you, Adam?"

"I am sent from heaven to help your children through the great darkness that is fast approaching." Adam's wool jacket was glowing a deep gold.

Kohler until now, was not a religious man, looked on in amazement. "Why have you come to me? I have never made a commitment to God. Why would God care what happens to me?"

"Because He has this night set His love upon you, Kohler. Take hold on it, and never let go. Now, I have other people I must attend to tonight."

Kohler looked down in thought for a couple seconds and would have spoken to Adam again, but he had vanished as silently as he had appeared. Before Kohler knew it, the door opened and Kohler was released. It seemed as if several hours were missing.

As he walked down the street that morning deep in thought about what had happened, a car pulled up to him. A kindly older man opened his window and asked if he would like a lift to where he was going. Kohler readily accepted, and he was soon home. He could not shake from his memory the events from the night before.

"What happened last night?" Richie asked his father.

"It was strange. I was taken to Berlin, and I met with a rather nasty Nazi officer who grilled me about something I wrote when I was in the Senate." He sighed and changed the subject. "I nearly jumped out of the car when you took out that side window last night. The driver was ashen the whole way to Berlin. What did you use?"

"The Mauser. The 8mm K98k I took home from the war," said Richie.

Adam stepped out of his room and went to the kitchen.

"Good morning Adam," Kohler greeted him.

Adam nodded and returned the greeting but spoke few words to Kohler. He had accomplished what he'd been sent to do, and there was nothing more that needed to be said at this time.

Later that day, an itinerant preacher made a stop in Luebben. He was preaching in the center of town, near the church. Out of curiosity, and with the events of the night before still fresh in his mind, Kohler went to speak to the preacher. "Sir, someone told me I needed to take hold on the gift of salvation. The problem is that I have never been a religious man."

"It is never too late, my friend," the preacher told him. The preacher read from his Bible the simple gospel message. *"Moreover, brethren, I declare unto you the gospel which I preached unto you, unless ye have believed in vain. For I delivered unto you first of all that which I also received, how that Christ died for our sins according to the*

scriptures: And that he was buried, and that he rose again the third day according to the scriptures."
(I Corinthians 15:1-4) The preacher finished with a prayer.

At once, it became clear to Kohler, and he responded to the call. He had never felt that way before, but suddenly he had a love for Christ and the God he hardly knew. He walked home a changed man.

Elizabeth noticed him walking down the lane with a smile on his face. "You went to see the preacher, didn't you?"

"Yes, I did. I can't explain what happened, but I began to feel love for God and for Christ who saved me. It's amazing, Elizabeth. Do you have a Bible I could borrow?"

Adam shouted a resounding "AMEN!" from his room.

"There is joy in the presence of the angels of God over the sinner that repenteth." (Luke 15:10)

Night came, and Elizabeth and Richie went as usual to the church, overjoyed at their father's sudden conversion to Christ. Sarah and David were already in the church with Gerhardt, looking over some other hymns he had written.

"Welcome," greeted Gerhardt. "Almost ready to start?"

"Yes we are." replied Richie

The evening hymn was *"Frohlich Soll Mein Herze Springen."* ("All My Heart with Joy is Springing.")

Gerhardt himself joined in with the singing. His voice blended beautifully with the others. The third verse hit Elizabeth particularly hard, as she thought about how she felt when her father was abducted the night before, and how she felt when he told her he had become a Christian.

"Christ our Lamb so meek and lovely,
Dries our tears, calms our fears, all our sins removing;
Christ our Lamb who suffers with us;
He can quell death and hell, and the peace restore us."

God had certainly dried her tears and removed all her fears, for the time being. There was a simple feeling of happiness every time she crossed the threshold of the church. How often she would remember the words of Psalm 122:1.

"I was glad when they said unto me, Let us go into the house of the Lord."

The Second Arrest

After singing that night, David asked Richie what he thought of the present political state of Germany, and particularly his opinion of the laws concerning the Jews. The question stunned Richie for a moment, then he noticed the glint of a gold pin on David's collar. The pin itself was hidden on the inside of the collar, but it was clear that David was working for the Nazi party.

Richie wisely told him he was still recovering from the war and did not yet have a solid opinion on the subject. He was glad he had been careful not to mention Adam, but he felt helpless. Would he slip and say something of his true feelings? A verse came to his mind from the book of Matthew 10:19: "*But when they deliver you up, take no thought how or what ye shall speak: for it shall be given you in that hour what ye shall speak . . .*"

David, however, seemed to be satisfied by his answer, and did not mention it again. It seemed to Richie that he was observing Richie's reaction to the question. Richie and Elizabeth hoped David would not be suspicious of them.

Walking home, Richie said, "That was close. The man is a Nazi. Did you know that?"

"No. I had no idea," Elizabeth sighed deeply. "But you know Richie, I still cannot believe that all these hymns are coming so easily. We have never harmonized together, and now, a few nights with this man who calls himself Paul Gerhardt, our four voices are beginning to blend flawlessly," said Elizabeth.

"Perhaps there is more to the man. Maybe he's the ghost of Paul Gerhardt," said Richie.

"Are you serious?" said Elizabeth.

"Perhaps, Elizabeth. It just seems that there is a supernatural aspect to the whole scene. Every time I pray with him, it feels like I am in Heaven, praising God in all His perfection. I've never felt that way before."

"Excuse me," came an unfamiliar voice behind them, "Are you Richie and Elizabeth Kohler?"

Richie and Elizabeth turned to see who spoke to them.

The man was pale and thin, wearing a long leather coat and a wool Fedora. Richie's heart began to pound. He took a step back. "Yes, I am Richie Kohler.

"I am Elizabeth Kohler. Who are you?"

"I am Carl Leider. You are friends, I believe, with my son, David."

"Yes, my friend Sarah Hess introduced David to us," Elizabeth said nervously.

"That's right," Leider said with a strange grin on his face.

She asked, "Is something wrong?"

"No, I don't think so," he shrugged, "I just had a report that a Jew had been seen at your door a few nights ago." Both Richie and his sister froze. "Of course, I know you wouldn't be that foolish," he said with a laugh, slapping Richie hard on the shoulder. Satisfied that he had successfully intimidated two helpless civilians, he turned and waltzed down the lane. His hellish laugh echoed ominously off the stone and brick houses that lined the street.

"David's father is with the Gestapo?" said Richie.

"What should we do now?" said Elizabeth.

Richie took a few deep breaths of the fresh night air. "Let's try to avoid talking politics with David anymore. I think they are onto us somehow."

About twelve-thirty that night, all was still in the house. The spring breeze blew gently through the open windows. Richie, a light sleeper, heard the screen door creak downstairs. As he walked quietly into the kitchen, the room appeared to be empty. He went to the door and looked out. Nothing. As he turned to walk away, Richie froze as a shapeless figure pressed the barrel of a handgun firmly against the back of his neck, in an upward position. Richie's hands shot up. He knew he had to be careful. The gun was positioned perfectly at his brain. Whoever it was knew what he was doing.

The stranger broke the silence by addressing him gruffly, but not loudly, so as not to wake the others. "Be very careful, Kohler. I have orders to arrest you or kill you if you resist. The choice is yours." Liquor effected the man's speech. Richie knew that the stranger could snap at any moment.

"Yes, I'll go with you."

The stranger withdrew the gun and replaced it inside his coat.

He seemed satisfied with Richie's attitude. "All right then," he said, putting a pair of handcuffs on his captive.

He put the cuffs on so tightly that they began to cut off Richie's circulation. His hands began to tingle and eventually went numb as the drunken stranger drove in the direction of Berlin, swerving as he went. Richie, who had felt afraid, at first, of getting into the car, now felt no fear. He strangely felt that there was someone sitting next to him, but the seat was empty.

A while later, they pulled up to a large brick building. Heavy bars secured the windows from the inside. Richie recognized the place as being the notorious Plotzensee Prison, a men's prison in Charlottenburg, a district of Berlin. His entire body went numb with a gripping fear. He was a strong young man, but nothing could have prepared him for this.

During the Nazi era, it was the largest prison in the German empire. It became notorious for being one of the main places for capital punishment. Over 2,800 prisoners were executed between 1937 and 1945. Many who stepped through its doors never came out alive.

The driver, who was not as intoxicated as he had been earlier, opened the door and pulled Richie out of the car. He was taken to an empty cell at the end of a long hallway. It was sparsely furnished with a cot and straight back chair. Richie thought that, at least, it was clean.

He sat on the hard cot and prayed a good while, after which his fears began to subside. As his eyes adjusted to the darkness, he became aware of someone standing near him. "Who are you?"

"I am Adam, Richie. Adam Engel. You were good enough to take me into your home when I came to your door. You do remember?"

"Yes. How did you get in here?"

Just then, a guard came by and opened the hatch. He shined his light around the room. "Who are you talking to, Crazy?" He laughed and slammed the hatch shut.

Richie was confused now. *How could the guard not see Adam standing next to him?* "Who are you, Adam?"

The room lit up in an incredible display of light, resembling a brilliant sunset. "I am an angel, Richie, sent by God. He sent me here to prepare you for the fast approaching trial that awaits you, and if needs be, take you home to Him."

Richie was stunned. "So that is why the pain from my injury left when we joined hands during the Passover prayer?"

"Yes. I will be with you in the morning. Prepare yourself, Richie. Now I must leave you. I have others who will be going home to God on the morrow. They must be prepared."

Adam turned and vanished through the brick wall. The light followed him as he walked silently down the gloomy halls, invisible to the guards posted at the corners.

The next morning, Richie was taken by two guards to an interrogation room down the hall. The room itself was plain but very neat. A bald man wearing a spotless SS uniform sat behind a neatly kept desk. A manila folder lay perfectly centered before him on the desk. He wore glasses and a hauntingly smug look on his face.

"Richard Kohler, age twenty-six," the man began to read, "Army sniper from 1942 to 1943, Honorable discharge for wounds received in the line of duty. Congratulations.

Outwardly, you seem to be the model soldier for the Reich."

"Outwardly?" asked Richie, confused by the man's emphasis on the word.

"Who are you trying to kid, Kohler? You were seen to accept a Jew into your home in Luebben at midnight a few days hence. Will you deny that?"

"Who would accuse me of such a thing? I will have his name!" Richie demanded.

The interrogator nodded and one of the guards forced Richie's hands down onto the table while the other pushed sewing needles under his fingernails. White hot pain shot through his entire body as he watched his nails turn dark blue.

"That is for your improper addressing of myself and for the death of Officer Schubert."

Richie wailed in pain and was sweating profusely.

The man nodded again, and the guard roughly removed the needles. "I'm sorry. I don't like it when people lie to me. It bothers me immensely.

Richie was trembling now. He knew there was no use trying to deny what they somehow already knew. He looked to his left. Standing next to the door was Adam. He wore a fine white linen suit. His very presence gave Richie the strength he needed.

"And there appeared an angel unto him from heaven, strengthening him." (Luke 22:43)

"Now, I will ask again, Kohler. Did you take a Jew into your home, or did you not?"

"No. It was a quick reaction. I saw someone in need, so I helped him. Only after did I realize he was a Jew. He left last night of his own accord."

"Good, good. Amazing what answers a little pain will get you."

"Sir, it was an honest mistake," Richie said in his own defense.

"You know, the Reich provides the death penalty for everyone who is caught giving aid to the Jews."

"But -" Richie started to protest.

"However," he said in a somewhat louder voice, raising his finger, "A man is entitled to a mistake—*one* mistake. I'm inclined to give you the benefit of the doubt. You can go home this time. I'm giving you a chance to live. That's very unusual, you understand. Normally, people who are brought here are executed within a few days."

"Thank you, I appreciate that," said Richie.

"As well you should. Now, before you return home, you will witness the deaths of twenty-five political prisoners who openly opposed the Reich. I sincerely hope you will take it to heart, and not make any more *mistakes*." He rose and shook Richie's hand. "Good day to you, Kohler."

Richie was escorted to the rear of the building and made to sit in a straight back chair. The guard next to him said, "I would advise you not to look away. Otherwise you will join these twenty-five. It will be over soon.

Twenty-five prisoners were led single file out the rear gate and lined up against an eight foot high wall. Each was given the option of a blindfold. One of the men, a weak old man with a long beard, held his hand to his heart and said, "Aim here." Some were indifferent to the fact their lives were about to end, while others trembled and prayed their final prayer, or cried for wives or mothers.

Before the execution, Richie saw something he would never forget. It was a dark, overcast day, and a light mist fell. All at once, the sky above the prisoners began to lighten. A large beam of deep golden light burst through the low clouds, filtered through the mist, and came to rest on twelve of the twenty-five men. In contrast, a dark shadow came over the other thirteen, as well as over the gunner who waited for the signal to fire. The stunning contrast between the light of God's love and the terrifying shadow of death for the thirteen who were not safe in Christ made Richie's blood run cold.

Seconds later it began. The signal was given, the safety released, and the deafening roll of the MG-34 echoing unbearably in Richie's ears as the wall behind the twenty-five men turned bright red as they fell, peppered with bullet holes. The light returned into the clouds, as did the mysterious dark shadow, and it was over. The guard standing next to Richie saw how it had affected him and said, "Kohler. It is over now. Time to go."

Richie looked at his hands. They trembled as they did every time he waited for a battle to begin.

The guard put Richie in a car and returned him to Luebben. He staggered from the car into the house and collapsed onto the floor. Elizabeth rushed to his aid and asked him what had happened. He told her he would share it with her after he rested. He spent the rest of the day in the confines of his room, emerging only after the last rays of sunshine had gone.

That evening Richie went to the church early to pray with his friend Paul. This simple act of worship melted his fears away. Paul said, "Be strong, my son. When you are weak in the flesh, let God be your strength by filling you with His Spirit. Never will He leave you. I have a hymn for you to learn tonight. I have called it: Awake, My Heart with Gladness. I hope you will like it."

Just then, the rest of the quartet came in through the old doors, and the lesson began.

As usual, the songs in the night formed effortlessly on their lips. They were ever mindful that God Himself was "teaching their tongues to sing."

"Awake, my heart, with gladness,
See what today is done;
Now, after gloom and sadness,
Comes forth the glorious Sun.

Our Saviour was laid
Where our bed must be made
When to the realms of light
Our spirit wings its flight . . . "

Verse after verse, they all sang with joy. A crippled old woman hobbled in and sat in the back of the church. By the time the third verse came around, she had her handkerchief out and was dabbing her eyes. She would later say that it was this same hymn that was sung at her husband's funeral in 1938. Words could not express her thankfulness for, as she put it, "a heavenly rendition" of the hymn. Such was often the case for those who would stop and listen for a verse or two. No matter who they were, all agreed it was beautiful music worthy of attention.

They sang the final verse for that evening,

"He brings me to the portal
that leads to bliss untold,
Whereon this rhyme immortal
is found in script of gold:
Who there my cross has shared
finds here a cross prepared;
Who there with me hath died
shall here be glorified."

Chapter 3

PASSING ALL UNDERSTANDING

Since the arrests, the daily life of Richie and Elizabeth grew more and more stressful. The angel, Adam, had taken his leave from the house. Things got worse when a little Jewish boy, starving and bruised, came knocking on their door one night. He was a lad forsaken by all. None would stop to help him for fear of being seen by those who may be working for the corrupt government, which could be anyone - children, shopkeepers, the little old lady next door, or even a "friend" like David. The Kohler's Christian faith left them no choice but to give food or shelter to all who knocked at their door, regardless of their religion, or the sinful laws that forbade them from providing for Jews.

The boy hadn't eaten in days. His clothes were torn, and his frail body covered with cuts and bruises. "We have no choice, " said Elizabeth with a quivering voice. "If we don't, it would be the same as if we didn't help Jesus himself."

Richie agreed. They had been tested by an angel, and they passed the test. Although clearly not another angel, the boy was yet another way God was testing them to see whether or not they would put their faith into action.

"For the poor shall never cease out of the land: therefore I command thee, saying, Thou shalt open thine hand wide unto thy brother, to thy poor, and to thy needy, in thy land." (Deuteronomy 15:11)

Richie gently helped the boy into the house and laid him on his own bed, as if in defiance of his personal fears and the trauma of the event he had just experienced. He had decided to set aside his own interests and look to help the interests of others.

"Look not every man on his own things, but every man also on the things of others." (Philippians 2:4)

Several weeks had now passed since the boy had been hiding in the Kohler's home in Luebben. It seemed to Elizabeth that everything was going to be all right, that the Gestapo would leave them alone. Such a thought was but a dream—a dream she continued to tell herself was true.

In Berlin, the SD (Security Service of the Reichsfuhrer-SS, the Intelligence Agency of the SS and the Nazi Party) had been feverishly collecting data on the Kohler siblings ever since Richie's arrest, and would soon be ready to close in on their prey. His unusual release from Plotzensee Prison was only meant to give him a little leash to see what direction he would go. As they suspected, he followed his heart.

~ ~ ~

One night, an angel of death came to visit Herr Kohler in his room. He stood by the window for a moment, and then walked confidently over to the head of the bed. He touched Kohler's shoulder and whispered, "Awake, you who sleep, and Christ will give you light."

Herr Kohler was instantly awakened by the voice that seemed to echo in the room. "Who are you? What are you doing in my house?"

"My name is Phillip. I'm an angel.. God's calling you home."

Herr Kohler was stunned. He had been saved only a short time, and now his life was about to end. "Why? My children, what will become of them?"

Philip gave him a sympathetic look and said, "Things are going to get extremely difficult for your children over the next couple of weeks, perhaps even deadly. Because of your weakness, and God's good pleasure, he is removing you from the heat of the coming spiritual war.

"So, what is the answer?"

"Herr Kohler, the Word of God says in Isaiah 57:1, *'The righteous perisheth, and no man layeth it to heart: and merciful men are taken away, none considering that the righteous is taken away from the evil to come.'*"

"Are my children not righteous?" Herr Kohler asked.

"They are," Philip assured him. "But it is God's purpose that they should touch the lives of others by their strength and selfless sacrifice, regardless of the cost. They will meet you again in heaven. Perhaps sooner than you think."

"Then I am ready."

Philip touched Herr Kohler on the shoulder, and he sank lifeless back onto the pillow.

During the funeral service at the Paul Gerhardt Church down the lane, both Elizabeth and Richie received a peace that surpassed all their understanding. A peace they would continue to lean upon in the coming days.

Chapter 4

TO BE WITH CHRIST IS FAR BETTER

It was now September, and the days were getting shorter. Sunlight temperatures were still in the seventies, while night lows dipped into the forties. The garden was still growing strong. Some of the early spring and summer plants had stopped producing, giving way to the more hearty varieties, such as carrots, beets, and turnips.

Richie stood in the garden hoeing potatoes. They were growing exceptionally well this year. A refreshing breeze blew across the garden and across Richie's face. He wiped his forehead on his sleeve and sighed, as he finished the last of the hoeing, rather pleased with himself. *"Now that's done."*

When Richie came in from the garden, Elizabeth was washing the dishes. Isaac. the little Jewish boy, dried them as fast as they came. They looked happy and content together. It was a beautiful sight. Aside from his religion, little Isaac was no different from any other boy his age. Elizabeth had even gone so far as to suggest they name him Isaac Kohler, but Richie declined. "I love the boy as much as you, but it would be too obvious. We have blond hair and blue eyes, classic Arian features, tall and good looking."

Elizabeth smiled at the comment.

"But Isaac has clear Jewish features, black hair, that big beak of a nose," he said, playfully pinching Isaac's nose, making him giggle gleefully. "It is enough that we are keeping him safe from the Nazis. He's already family. Richie began to quote a verse, *"Feed the flock of God which is among you . . ."*

To Richie's surprise, Isaac quoted the rest of the verse with him. *"taking the oversight thereof, not by constraint, but willingly..."* (1 Peter 5:2)

"Where did you learn that, little brother?" asked Richie.

"I heard it from an old man at the church down the street. He gave me something to eat and then sent me here."

Richie knew it must have been Gerhardt. Who else would have known their secret ministry? He allowed himself no further uneasiness about it.

Every night Richie and Elizabeth went to the church for choral practice. They left Isaac hiding in the closet under the stairs with a few children's books and a small torch for light.

As the weeks passed, the choral group became better and better at mastering their own parts in harmony. What would turn out to be the last song they would sing together was one of Gerhardt's most beautiful hymns, *"O Jesu Christ, Mein Schonstes Licht"* ("Jesus, Thy Boundless Love to Me.")

"O grant that nothing in my soul,
May dwell but thy pure love alone;
O, may thy love possess me whole,
My joy, my treasure, and my crown!
All coldness of my heart remove;
My every act, word, thought, be love."

The entire sanctuary had a heavenly presence that night, something neither Richie nor Elizabeth had ever experienced. It was that same presence they would feel again in just two days.

The next day went by strangely fast, and Richie had lost his appetite. Throughout the day, both he and Elizabeth subconsciously let go of all earthly attachments. Especially

Richie. Worldly things he cared about now meant nothing. He could think of nothing but being forever the presence of God. They thought it strange that suddenly two people in the flower of life were losing the love for their own life. God was preparing them for Richie's homegoing.

That night, when they went to the church, Sarah and David were not there. The church was dark, save for the flicker of a few candles at the altar. Paul came out from behind the curtain and said, "I thought we would just pray together this evening." His voice was solemn and caring. The hour of prayer went by far too quickly, but alas, the time came to return home. Paul sent them away with a blessing.

Neither Richie nor Elizabeth slept that night, yet they were not tired when morning came. Throughout the night, Richie heard heavenly singing that wafted in on the breeze.

At six o'clock that morning, members of the Gestapo met in Berlin to plan the raid that was to take place at ten o'clock sharp. Weeks earlier, they had given the old woman down the lane a good deal of money to watch the Kohler house, and it paid off. She was a night owl and was reading by the window when the boy had come to the Kohler's door. She saw Richie accept him inside. Warrants had been issued for the arrests of Elizabeth and Richie.

At ten sharp, Richie was working in the garden. He froze and dropped his hoe at the sight of two Volkswagen military vehicles rattling up the lane. He was afraid, but had been expecting this moment since his arrest weeks ago. The vehicles stopped in front of the house and several soldiers jumped out and surrounded the house. Two stood guard at the door as the officer in charge, knocked calmly on the door.

They could hear Elizabeth humming as she came to the door. The officer, Sergeant Schmidt, grinned to the guard next to him, nodded and said, "She has no idea." As soon as she opened the door, she put her hand to her mouth and gasped, speechless. Schmidt roughly pushed her out of the way. She tripped over the rug and fell on the floor. A set of powerful arms quickly lifted her up and sat her in a chair. Schmidt wore glasses, a crisp gray uniform. His hat, with the Nazi eagle and swastika, had under the iconic emblem, the notorious silver skull. His face bore all the stress and strain that came with being a veteran of the party's military wing, and now a man in charge. His blue eyes were cold as ice. "Where are you hiding your Jew?"

"I don't know what you're-"

She was cut short by a powerful backhand slap on the cheek.

She tottered, bracing herself against the arm of the chair. She cried out, "Jesus, Help Me!"

Trembling. Richie had now been brought in and made to sit down on the other side of the living room.

"I ask you again, Fraulein. Where are you hiding the boy? He was seen to come here in the middle of the night and has not left. Where?"

"I have told you, sir. I don't-"

"Stop!" he ordered, "I really do not like it when people lie to me. Now, I ask you again, where is your Jew?"

Elizabeth shook her head, followed by another hard slap. Elizabeth was now bleeding from the nose from the force of the blows and held her handkerchief to her face until it stopped. " Fraulein, I ask-" The officer would have continued, but he was interrupted.

"Never mind, sir," came the voice of the other officer.. "Look what I found hiding in the closet like a serpent in the boughs." A rather large and homely soldier had his big, strong hands on Isaac's small shoulders. Nearly suspending him in midair, he dragged Isaac into the living room with the rest of the group.

"Take him to the gardening shed, and make it go away." the officer ordered.

A few moments later, Elizabeth heard a brief scream and two muffled shots in the shed. She could not control her sobbing.

Richie tried to make a move on the officer in charge, but he was instantly struck down by the butt of a rifle. Adrenaline prevented the pain from coming through, and he quickly regained his composure. Like a flash, he caught the soldier who hit him completely off guard. Richie shot him with the guard's own rifle, along with two others before he was subdued.

Schmidt was stunned at Richie's apparent superhuman strength. "As much as it hurts me to say, Kohler, you will not be accompanying your sister to Berlin this morning . . . Take him out back."

Phillip and Adam stood at the door of the gardening shed, glowing with a light so bright that it illuminated the area around the shed. Phillip addressed him kindly, stretching out his arm and helping him up the steps of the shed. "I am Phillip. I took your father, and I'm here to take you. Your Lord is calling you home. You have done well." Richie knelt on the bloody floor next to the body of little Isaac. He prayed while the soldier tilted his head forward. He heard the hammer drop, and it was over.

Phillip helped Richie to his feet and a burst of light changed everything around him. No more gardening shed. It was replaced by a gate of pure gold leading to the Celestial City directly in front of him. Richie was finally home in joy unspeakable.

"And God shall wipe away all tears from their eyes; and there shall be no more death, neither sorrow, nor crying, neither shall there be any more pain; for the former things are passed away." (Revelation 21:4)

Elizabeth was arrested and tried in Berlin. However, when she stood before the People's Court, a look of utter surprise came over the judge's face. The judge read the verdict which was written by someone high up in the Reich government. She had been given a rare but welcomed pardon. The judge smiled and said, "Fraulein Kohler, you are pardoned. You are free to go." She stood stunned for a moment.

Elizabeth sold the house in Luebben and disappeared deep in the mountains of Prague. She remained there until the end of the war.

"The Lord will command his lovingkindness in the daytime, and his song in the night shall be with me, and my prayer unto the God of my life." (Psalm 42:8)

Das Ende

ANGELS OF THE THIRD REICH: SONGS IN THE NIGHT II

BOOK THREE

Berlin, Germany
June, 1944

"He hath put a new song in my mouth, even praise unto our God . . . " (Psalm 40:3)

"My Saviour, be thou near me when death is at my door:
Then let thy presence cheer me, forsake me never more."
                              Paul Gerhardt, 17th Century

Chapter 1

THE ASSIGNMENT

Martin Graf and Margaret Kruger were students at the University of Berlin Surgical Clinic, where they studied the latest in experimental surgery and medical procedures. The Dean of the college, Eugene Fischer, was a vicious and passionate supporter of the Nazi regime. Fischer quickly fired or expelled all those who opposed Hitler. The Jewish professors or teachers who once walked the old halls, do so no longer. The new, better education of the Third Reich replaced the teachings of old Germany. Germany's messiah, Hitler had not led them into peace, but war.

Now, during the final two years of the war, several failed attempts were made on Adolf Hitler's life. The attempts on his life caused Hitler to hide himself in his private housing, only seeing his trusted advisors. For some time, members of the military who opposed Hitler's actions and policies were planning an attempt they thought sure would finally work to end the reign of terror. This attempt was known as *Operation Valkyrie.*

"My, that breeze sure feels good," said Margaret as she and her friend, Martin, stepped onto the grass after the afternoon recess bell.

"That it does. Pretty stuffy in that classroom if you ask me." said Martin.

"Helps you concentrate, I think," said Margaret.

Martin laughed at the thought of his eccentric old teacher.

As they spoke and enjoyed the air, two people approached the college. "Excuse me. Can you direct us to the office of the Dean - Dean Fischer, I believe?"

Martin said, "Yes, of course. Straight through the double doors and to the left . . . though I don't think you'll be there very long."

"Oh? Why is that?" asked David.

"Because he hates Jews."

David was a handsome Jewish man in his late twenties. "Thanks for the tip, though I don't think it'll be a problem. I am David, by the way. This is my friend Barbara." They all shook hands.

"I'm sure we'll be seeing more of you in the weeks to come. Barbara and I are going to be students in Herr Hoffman's medical class. Good day to you both."

Martin watched as the new students climbed the stairs and walked through the doors. "Is it just me, or did that girl have a grip like you've never felt before?"

"Bless the Lord, ye his angels, that excel in strength, that do his commandments, hearkening unto the voice of his word." (Psalm 103:20)

"I'll say. For that matter, so did he. I wonder where they are from?"

"Not sure," said Martin staring back at the college. "Not sure."

The rest of the day went by smoothly and before they knew it, the bell rang and school was let out.

Barbara and David again approached and asked Margaret if she knew of a good place to lodge for the next few weeks.

"We have a large apartment quite near here. There are a couple extra bedrooms we could set up for you."

Barbara accepted without hesitation. She and David moved in that day. They travelled very light, carrying only one small suitcase each.

Margaret silently observed Barbara and her friend that evening. She noticed Barbara and David both wore the same style ring. The design was two Seraphim - their wings surrounding a bright, radiant cut diamond. The sides were embossed with a lion in full roar. The design suggested royalty, but Margaret did not ask about the rings, as she thought it was none of her business.

That night, Barbara took it upon herself to work in the kitchenette, where she happily washed the dishes. She began to hum as she washed, and soon started to sing. Her voice carried into the den, where Margaret sat in a comfortable chair studying. She stopped to listen for a moment. She smiled and wished that she could sing that way. Martin and David were sitting having light conversation.

Barbara soon emerged from the kitchenette and asked, "Would you have time to show us around a little? I'd love to see some of the local sights."

Martin told her that the St. Nicholas Church was a beautiful example of German architecture.

"Could we go see it now, Martin?"

"Ready when you are."

The night air was pleasantly warm. As the four students walked to the church, a feeling of peace and happiness came over Martin. Something rather unusual when the whole of Europe was deeply engulfed in the Second World War.

They made it to the church and found it unlocked. The priest was working that night on something in the basement. Martin asked if he could show his friends the church and the priest smiled. "Of course. You may show your friends the church any time. I'll be here for a while."

Barbara was drawn to a large frame on the wall. It contained a Latin text that no one in the church had ever translated into song.

"This is interesting." Barbara began to translate: *O Jehovah, be gracious unto us; we have waited for thee: be thou our arm every morning, our salvation in the time of trouble.* That is from Isaiah 33:2," she said.

Looking through a hymn book laying open on the ornate pulpit, Barbara turned to page 412 and began to sing the words to a song written by Bernard of Clairvaux in the Twelfth Century.

David fell into effortless harmony as they sang a verse together.

"Jesus, thou joy of loving hearts,
Thou fount of life, Thou light of men,
From the best bliss that earth imparts,
We turn to Thee unfilled again."

Martin was amazed at the beauty and volume of their voices as they echoed through the empty church.

Margaret sat in one of the pews listening to the singing. This hymn was sung at the funeral of her beloved grandfather in early 1940. He had taken his own life after learning that his entire family including his wife had been executed by the Nazis in Warthegau, a Polish province. Tears filled her eyes. The hymn brought back memories of her grandfather and the emotions of day when she was notified by a local officer that he had died.

"Why did you stop?" asked Margaret.

"Come up here," Barbara motioned with a kindly smile.

Martin and Margaret walked to the front and up the steps to the pulpit.

"Tonight," said David, "we are going to teach you both how to sing. God has given everyone a voice by which he may praise his Creator. Music will sustain you in times of diversity and emotional stress and bring you joy."

David first asked Martin to sing a little, but Martin struggled to keep the tune. "Martin, concentrate on keeping your voice box lower in your throat."

"How am I supposed to do that?" asked Martin.

"Push your tongue back in your mouth, and you will do it automatically." David gave him a note to try and then said, "Hold it."

Martin was surprised how easy it was.

"The hardest part for you is to be able to hear the different parts of the harmony. Now let us try this first verse again." He put his hand on Martin's shoulder and prayed aloud for him. "Our Father, come and touch the voice of this fine young man, and show him your great love. Hold him by Jesus, in Thy right hand."

For the first time in his life, Martin was able to sing without putting strain on his throat. He was also surprised to find himself falling into his part of the harmony. It wasn't perfect, but it was an encouraging start.

Over the next few days, the students practiced each night. Soon they were able to project their four voices which blended flawlessly. Now and then, a passing policeman or private citizen would pause and listen to what some called, the voices of angels. Perhaps it was an angelic blessing. The acapella singing served as a respite each night from the constant dread of the war which had now spread from Germany all the way to Japan.

Chapter 2

THE SECOND SEAL

Tensions rose every time the air raid alarm was tested or a plane flew overhead. Children could be seen crying in fear outside in their yards. Even Margaret would find herself scanning the sky and the horizon looking for enemy planes. Often at night, she would turn on the wireless and hear rumors that Royal Air Force Bases were stocked with D-A 20s aimed directly at Hitler's occupied territories. Her heart would pound as she took in all the news.

Hearing all these reports, Martin nervously wrung his hands and walked about the apartment. This made Margaret even more nervous.

Barbara sat down next to her and said, "You know, you really don't need to listen to that kind of thing. God has promised never to leave or forsake you, especially in those times when you need him most. The world is at war, Margaret. God is not going to leave you at a time like this. This is when He steps in and takes over. It's time you started taking Him at His word. God says, "*I will not leave you comfortless: I will come to you. . . the Comforter, which is the Holy Ghost, whom the Father will send in my*

name, he shall teach you all things. My peace I give unto you: not as the world giveth, give I unto you. Let not your heart be troubled, neither let it be afraid."
(John 14:18, 26, 27)

The words cut deeply into Margaret's troubled heart. She had allowed herself to be troubled and afraid and she was trembling.

Barbara said, "Look what your needless worry has done." She smiled and touched Margaret on the shoulder.

The moment Barbara touched her, Margaret was filled with a peace and warmth that coursed through her entire body. "It's hard for me to let go. I have never really made a commitment to God. Why would He really care about one college student among hundreds of others?"

"Because that is how He works. He elects a few and sets them apart to be used for His own will," said Barbara.

David had been listening to the conversation and said, "You know Margaret, when the Second Seal is opened, there will be no use worrying about what happens afterward. It's all in God's plan."

"Second Seal?" asked Margaret.

David spoke in a hauntingly deep voice. "Yes, that is when peace is taken from the earth and people will kill one another." David quoted, *"And when he had opened the second seal, I heard the second beast say, come and see. And there went out another horse that was red: and power was given to him that sat thereon to take peace from the earth, and that they should kill one another, and there was given unto him a great sword.* That is from the Book of The Revelation, Chapter 6, verses 3 and 4."

Margaret's blood ran cold. She was shocked that it sounded so much like the current state of the entire world.

Suddenly, there was a knock on the apartment door. Martin looked at his watch. It was eight-thirty. "Who could that be at this time of night?" he asked, assuming it was probably the Gestapo coming to ask about the new students.
Sure enough, two men wearing business suits stood in the doorway.

"Yes sir? Can I help you?" asked Martin.

"We have information that you have two new students staying with you. Is that true?"

"Yes, it is. They arrived a couple of days ago. They're taking the same classes, so we shared our rooms."

"We have orders to take them for questioning," said one of the agents.

Barbara and David stepped forward and approached the agents confidently. "What do you want from us?" asked David, looking the agent straight in the eyes.

"Just your cooperation. Nothing more."

The agent took a step backward. There was something about their presence that made him very uneasy, though he had no apparent reason for such feelings.

"Why are you so nervous?" David asked, taking another step forward.

"I don't know what you're talking about," the agent said with a nervous tone of voice.

David looked, as if at the sky, and then back at the agent.

A rumble of thunder was heard in the distance. The agent looked at his partner and said, "I see there is nothing to worry about here. *Gute Nacht.*" They left abruptly.

"What was that all about?" asked Martin. "I thought they were going to take you with them."

"We persuaded them otherwise," said David. "You know, I think I will retire now. I will see you two in the morning."

Several days passed without any more trouble from curious security agents, and classes seemed more interesting. Each night after class, the four students walked to the church and sang together for an hour. Martin and Margaret found their parts in the harmony and were now able to project their voices effortlessly. The words of the great hymn writer, Paul Gerhardt resonated through the empty sanctuary that evening.

"Why should cross and trial grieve me?
Christ is near, with his cheer,
Never will he leave me.
Who can rob me of the heaven
That God's son for me won
When his life was given.
God gives me my days of gladness,
And I will trust him still
When he sends me sadness.
God is good; his love attends me,
Day by day, come what may,

Guides me and attends me.
Now in Christ, death cannot slay me,
Though it might, day and night,
Trouble and dismay me.
Christ has made my death a portal
From the strife of this life
To his joy immortal."

The only other person in the church that night was a man who cleaned and kept the shrubs pruned. He paused from his work and sat in a pew at the back. "That was beautiful! It was just what I needed tonight. Thank you."

It was that night that God called both Martin and Margaret. For the last few days, David and Barbara had been explaining the need of salvation through Christ. As Martin and Margaret walked out of the church, they were suddenly overcome with a need for God. So much so that they fell to their knees sobbing. David knelt beside them and ministered to them. Soon they would find that salvation had come at just the right time.

During the next few days, the other students in Martin's class asked what was different about him and Margaret, for they had seen the sudden change. Martin responded by saying that they had finally found what they had needed–peace in the midst of the war.

Chapter 3

THE FURNACE OF AFFLICTION

It was Tuesday, July 19th. The sun rose early over Berlin, but soon gave way to clouds. Throughout the day, Martin could not shake the heavy feeling that had beset him. He prayed often in the day, and found that prayer alone brought him peace, a sanctuary into which he could retire as often as he wished without fear of being troublesome to God.

Some of the students had been acting strangely for the past couple of days. Leaving during lunch hour, being distant from everyone and wearing a solemn face. As it turned out, they had been attending meetings with high ranking military personnel to plan an assassination attempt on Hitler. Martin himself had strong feelings about Hitler's abuse of power. The mass genocide of an innocent race of people greatly angered him. He thought it best however, to keep his feelings quiet when he was at the college. The Dean would expel any who opposed Hitler.

July 20th dawned a beautiful day. The golden sunbeams filtered through the trees which were filled with rain drops from the storm the night before, and the entire city of Berlin was aglow like the celestial city.

Classes came and went in a daze for Martin. He ate hardly anything all day and spent class breaks at his desk. Something had changed. Throughout the day, he would hear waves of what he described in his journal as "Heavenly" singing, music and harmonies more beautiful than he had ever heard. He noticed it seemed the opposite for Margaret. To her the lessons were enjoyable and clear. She appeared to have an overall sense of well-being.

Around 1:30, a commotion spread through the college students and teachers alike. Some were crying and some were shouting. Dean Fischer called the students into the assembly room and declared that Hitler had been killed at his Wolf's Lair Headquarters in the deep Masurian Forests in Poland.

School was let out early that day, and everyone walked about in a daze, shocked at the devastating news. But within hours, reports came in and were confirmed that Hitler was not dead. He was injured and livid, sustaining only a few minor cuts and a perforated eardrum. He had ordered the arrest and execution of all those directly or even remotely connected with the attack and initiation of *Operation Valkyrie*.

Over the course of a few short months, more than seven thousand people were arrested by the Gestapo. Of these, about five thousand were executed in various prisons around Germany. Two of Martin's friends were also executed. They were not directly part of the attack but had been outspoken against Hitler's abuse of authority. They were cunning young men. The Gestapo had never been able to find enough evidence to hold them longer than 48 hours. But now with the botched assassination attempt, the Gestapo had *carte blanche* on arresting whomever they wished. Many did so to settle old debts and get revenge for personal reasons. Martin's friends were killed as a personal vendetta for inconvenience.

Three days after the attempted assassination on Hitler, there was a knock at the door around eleven P.M. The sound of heavy pounding on the apartment door startled Martin out of a sound sleep. He looked at his watch and noted the time. "God help me!" he prayed under his breath as he walked swiftly to the front door. As he expected, there were two men in long leather coats standing before him.

"Martin Graf, you must come with us," said one of the agents.

"Will you give me enough time to pack an overnight bag?"

One of the men nodded and said, "Be quick about it, won't you?"

They stepped into the dimly lit living room and waited as Martin quickly stuffed a few things into a bag. He trembled and uttered verses to himself to try and stay calm, "*Behold, I have refined thee, but not as silver. I have chosen thee in the furnace of affliction.*" (Isaiah 48:10)

"I am ready now," Martin addressed the officers.

"Thank you for your cooperation, Heir Graf. You keep this up and you *may* be returning home tonight." The two men led Martin down the stairs to a waiting car. After a short ride, they arrived at the front of Plotzensee Prison.

He prayed as he went through the door of the prison. "Hold me, Father. Hold me by my right hand and help me."

"For I the Lord thy God will hold thy right hand, saying unto thee, fear not; I will help thee." (Isaiah 41:13)

There was no waiting. Martin was taken directly into interrogation. As Martin and the officer walked to the room, they passed a man in his mid-thirties sitting on a bench. He looked up briefly at Martin as he passed. He said nothing, but somehow, Martin heard a voice behind him say, "It is I; be not afraid. I will never leave you nor forsake you."

Martin was startled. When he looked back at the man there was nothing but an empty bench. Only a second or two had passed, and there was nowhere for the stranger to go but down the long, narrow hallway. He could not help consider that he might have seen his Saviour fulfilling His promise in a very personal way.

The interrogation room was small and thick with fragrant pipe smoke. A lamp stood on the desk, the bulb facing Martin. Behind the littered desk sat a man with a crisp white shirt and thick glasses. "Thank you for coming, Heir Graf," he greeted, taking a thin manila file out of the drawer. "This shouldn't take long."

A voice within Martin told him not to speak, so he remained silent.

The man stared at him for a few silent moments and then introduced himself. "My name is Reinhart Eckert, Martin. I've been doing this for a long time. I have had many men executed starting back in the late thirties. If there is no evidence, you will be returning home in the morning. But if the evidence suggests that you were in any way involved in the assassination attempt on the twentieth of July, you will be killed."

"I understand," Martin said, nervously rubbing his forehead. He began quoting a verse to himself. *"But when they deliver you up, take no thought how or what ye shall speak: for it shall be given you in that same hour what ye shall speak."* (Matthew 10:19)

For three straight hours, Eckert asked question after question, and continued to produce faulty evidence and concluded that Martin was somehow involved. It became clear to Martin that he would not leave the prison alive.

Throughout the night, Martin learned the true depth of cruelty of his interrogator, Eckert. Every time Eckert asked a question, Martin would have to think carefully before he spoke. If he should answer wrong, he might get a backhand or a needle driven under his fingernails.

"Pain is one of my best methods," Eckert said laughing as Martin trembled in pain sweating profusely. "It makes a man sing like a canary and tell me anything I want to know."

"How can I do that when I don't know what you want me to tell you?" Martin pleaded.

"Everything. I want you to tell me everything. Hold nothing back."

"I have told you everything. I had nothing to do with the attempted assassination. I am apolitical. Just because my friends happened to be part of it does not mean that I was."

Eckert shook his head. "I think the opposite. I think that a man is known by the company he keeps. I think they confided in you and told you some of their secrets and perhaps some names of others involved. The leaders have already been shot: Stauffenburg, Beck, and others."

Martin found no words to say, so he kept silent.

"Well, aren't you going to answer me? Have you no words in your defense? It's looking rather grim, wouldn't you say?"

"I have told you what I know. I have no ties with any conspirators. That is all. I am finished talking with you."

Eckert nodded and sighed. "Alright." He closed the file and put it into a cabinet. Another case was finished.

Martin knew that by refusing to say more, he had signed his own death warrant, but there is only so much a man can do to convince another of his innocence.

"You will face the People's court and from there be taken to a place of execution."

"*In deine Hande Herr, meinen Geist I*," Martin said under his breath. "Into thine hand O Lord, I commit my spirit."

Eckert nodded to the guard waiting at the door. "Take him away."

When the room was empty, Eckert poured himself a shot of whiskey that he kept under the desk. He knocked it back and uttered a satisfied, "Ahh! whiskey makes everything better."

The room was dark except for the dim light produced by the small desk lamp. He leaned back in his chair and stared out the window, gently turning his second shot in the glass. Suddenly, a voice called his name. "Eckert."

Startled, he dropped the glass. Before him stood a young man wearing a spotless white cotton suit. "Who are you?" Eckert demanded.

David stepped closer. "My name is David. You have killed your last man in Martin Graf."

"What the hell are you talking about? You have no idea what you're talking about!"

"I beg to differ. I have been sent to take Martin home."

"Graf is going nowhere. Do you understand? NOWHERE, DAMN IT!" he shouted, so loud that a guard came in to check.

"Sir? Are you all right? Who are you talking to?"

"What? The man standing next to you, of course!" shouted Eckert. The guard turned pale and left, for he could not see David.

"Who are you?" Eckert asked, having briefly composed himself.

"I am an angel of death. Your time, sir, is also running out. You will not see the end of the war."

Eckert laughed nervously and said, "Y-you are a very troubled young man who needs psychological help, nothing more."

The room instantly lit up in deep gold and engulfed David. "Repent and turn from your sin before it is too late, Eckert. The next angel you see will not reveal to you the glory of God, but His wrath." David turned and vanished through the oak door.

Eckert punctured a cyanide capsule in his mouth and took his own life. His ungodly remorse for his many sins had brought him to a sudden and bitter end.

Chapter 4

MARTIN'S HOME-GOING

Barbara offered to drive Margaret to see Martin at the Plotzensee Prison. I'm sure they took him there," she said as they rounded the corner and came within sight of the prison. After Margaret went through the heavy doors, David came and sat with Barbara. The guard took Margaret down to the cell to see Martin. The cell was small but clean.

"Margaret!" Martin said, getting up to meet his friend.

Tears fell from Margaret's eyes as she saw him through the bars.

"Are they treating you well?" Margaret asked.

"No. But it should not be long, I think," said Martin.

"No, don't say that. You are my best friend." Margaret sobbed.

"It's okay. We will see each other again in heaven." They spoke for a few minutes and Margaret left.

As Margaret came through the door, David told Barbara and Margaret, "I have to go. See you later this evening."

Regardless of the heartbreak of losing her best friend to the Nazis, Margaret continued to sing with David and Barbara at the church. One night, David began to sing a song that Margaret had never heard, and Barbara soon fell into harmony. They had no lyrics or music, but Margaret found herself singing the words.

"Rejoice my heart, be glad and sing
A cheerful trust maintain;
For God, the source of everything,
Thy portion shall remain
He is thy treasure, he thy joy
Thy life and light and Lord,
Thy counselor when doubts annoy,
Thy shield and great reward.
Why spend the day in blank despair,
If restless tho't the night?
On thy Creator cast thy care:
He makes thy burden light.
Did not His love and pow'r
Watch o'er thy childhood day?
Has he not in threat'ning hour
Turned dreaded ills away?" *(Paul Gerhardt)*

"What's happening to me? I have never heard these words before, but they came so easily," Margaret asked after they finished. Barbara smiled warmly.

Late that night, Margaret stood at the kitchenette sink looking out the window. She loved that window, with its view of the park beyond. The moon rose brightly over the dark silhouette of the tree line. Something caught her attention in the far corner of the park, partially obscured by a large willow tree. It was Barbara and David. They were standing together and seemed to be deep in conversation. She watched them carefully as they occasionally looked up into the starlit heavens.

Margaret reached for a dish towel, but it slipped out of her hands. She bent down to retrieve it and returned to her dishes. When she looked again, the scene below had changed. The entire area of the park where Barbara and David stood was engulfed in a soft golden light that seemed to be coming from the North. Margaret then realized that for the past several weeks, she had been interacting with God's heavenly messengers.

Suddenly, Margaret heard heavy knocking at the door. Startled, she dropped a plate and quickly dried her hands. A cold sweat formed on her brow as she slowly made her way to the door.

"Margaret?" came a voice from behind her.

Margaret gasped. Barbara stood in the kitchen doorway wearing a crisp, white skirt suit. "Don't answer that yet."

"Why?" asked Margaret.

"The Gestapo believes you had knowledge of the attack on Hitler and were part of it in some way." said Barbara.

"What? No, I knew nothing about it," said Margaret.

"I know that," said Barbara

"I-I saw you out in the park with David," Margaret stuttered.

"Yes. I know. You need to pull yourself together. Do you understand?"

The knocking continued and was now coupled with threats to break down the door.

"We don't have long so listen carefully. You need to pack a travel bag right now and follow me to the car. Go!" Barbara spoke with authority.

Margaret trembled as she gathered a few things from her closet. Barbara stood by the door. When Margaret came out, Barbara motioned for Margaret to stand next to her.

Seconds later, the door was kicked off its hinges and SS officers burst in carrying weapons. "Are you Margaret Anne Kruger?" one of the men asked her.

"Y-yes, I am," answered Margaret.

"We have orders to take you for questioning in connection with the July 20 assassination attempt on the Fuhrer. Do you have anything to say before your arrest?"

"I have," said Barbara, standing undaunted beside Margaret. "She is going nowhere with you."

The officer grinned and motioned for two of the officers to arrest Barbara as well. When they approached, she raised her hands toward heaven and a broad flash of light that resembled lightning burst through the ceiling and lit up the entire room for a split second. A couple of windows shattered from the force of this mysterious light. The officers fell backward and were flattened to the floor. Their eyes were severely bloodshot as they stood up and stumbled to find the door.

"And they smote the men that were at the door of the house with blindness, both small and great: so that they wearied themselves to find the door." (Genesis 19:11)

Barbara took on a heavenly glow and said, "Margaret, God has sent us to take you to safety. Quickly, follow me." At the street level, Barbara opened the back door of a comfortable black coup parked at the curb.

"Wait, what about Martin?" Margaret asked.

"God is calling him home in the morning. Do not worry. David is with him now. Come."

Barbara headed in the direction of Central Poland, which now had been liberated by the Russians.

They passed through three checkpoints without stopping. In fact, the guards did not even look up. Margaret was amazed to see God working to bring her to safety. Margaret was taken to a Russian post and then taken out of the occupied counties. She lived in Geneva until the end of the war. Even though content with the life God had given her now, she still thought about the events she had witnessed during the war: the angels, the blinding of the SS officers, the heavenly singing, and the tragic loss of her friend, Martin

Graf. He would always hold a special place in Margaret's heart.

~ ~ ~

Meanwhile, Martin tossed and turned all night on the uncomfortable cot in his cell, thinking about eternity, life, death, judgement, and his salvation, which he felt sure was secure in Christ.

"Martin," came a voice from behind him. He turned to see David standing beside the small, barred window. David wore a white linen suit.

"Why are you all dressed up?" asked Martin.

"Because I am going to take you to your heavenly home in the morning."

Martin said, "That's a job for an angel of death, not a college student. I always knew there was something different about you."

David smiled and the cell was instantly flooded with heavenly golden light. "I am an angel of death, Martin. God is calling you home."

Martin broke down as his fear gave way to peace and joy. "Then I just want to go home," he said with tear-filled eyes.

David gave him words of comfort. "I'll see you in the morning." David walked out of the cell through the wall and into the courtyard.

Morning came quickly. Martin had slept peacefully. He now faced the People's Court for a very brief sentencing. From there, he was taken to the work shed in back of the prison. David and another angel dressed in a suit of brilliant white stood on the platform on either side of the Fallbeil. The Fallbeil was Germany's version of the French Guillotine. Martin was placed in stocks and positioned with his head under the blade. Within seconds, the safety was released. The 16 inch, 125 pound blade fell and Martin was home in the presence of the God he loved.

"The Lord will command his lovingkindness in the daytime, and his song in the night shall be with me, and my prayer unto the God of my life." (Psalm 42:8)

Das Ende

ANGELS OF THE THIRD REICH: BELGIUM RESISTANCE

BOOK FOUR

Student Hostel,
Italielei 237,
Antwerpen, Belgium.
May 1943

Chapter 1

ANDREW HEIDEN'S HOME-GOING

It was Friday, May 20th. The sun rose with a heavenly glow. Its warm rays through the bedroom window were dancing off Emily Heiden's face. Within a few minutes after waking up, the sun disappeared behind a thick blanket of clouds.

While Emily was having breakfast with a couple of other students at the hostel, she heard a knock at the door. It was her longtime friend, Officer Peter Beck. He had been a Belgium Police officer for about five years and now wore the symbol of the Nazi dictatorship that ruled Germany with an iron fist. Regardless of the eagle and swastika on his sleeve, underneath he was still the same Peter that she grew up with, running through the streets of old Antwerp.

The look on Peter's face immediately told Emily that he was not on a social call. With tears in his eyes he struggled to speak. "Emily, it's about your father."

"What is it?" Emily asked, her voice now riddled with panic. "Peter Beck, you tell me what's going on!" Her voice cracked, realizing that something was very wrong.

"Andrew Heiden is at the Fort of Breendonk. The officer

in charge ordered me to bring you there." Peter led her to his car and they left for the twenty-five minute ride from Antwerp to Breendonk.

The trip went by quickly in silence. As they rounded the corner, the fortress came into view, surrounded by green grass and its wide mote. As they crossed the bridge and drove through the first stone archway, fear began to set into Emily's bones. This was the kind of fear that cripples and makes your hands tremble. Two stern looking guards with their German Shepherds approached the car and promptly asked for Peter's ID, which he held out the window.

One of the guards took the ID, glanced at it and returned his papers saying, "All right, Beck, go ahead."

"Thank you, sir."

The other guard grinned wickedly at Emily and winked.

Emily looked down, a little frightened. She had heard stories about Nazi officers and young girls. She was relieved when the guard told Peter he could go.

Peter drove to the main entrance where two soldiers stood guard at either side of a heavy wooden door that had darkened with age. The door creaked like a prison door out of the French Revolution. A soldier led Emily down into the basement of the fort. He gently sat her down in a plain wooden chair in front of a large window that separated the room from the next room. A heavy black curtain obscured the view from the window between the rooms. A speaker in the corner of the room began to play the second movement of Chopin's Minute Waltz.

Moments later the curtain was drawn back and Emily nearly passed out.

Her father had his hands tied behind him, and the handcuffs were attached to a heavy galvanized chain suspended from the ceiling. At one end of the window there was a small sound hole so Emily could hear what was happening. An interrogator began to ask Andrew questions about his involvement with the British Navy and other activities. Emily got the impression that her father may have been involved in espionage or selling information about German military movements to enemies of the Third Reich.

Things started to get serious when Andrew claimed he didn't know what they were talking about. A guard entered the room and began to slowly tighten the chain. In a very short time, Andrew screamed in mortal agony. The muscles in his arms, sides and shoulders were torn as the chains tightened notch by notch. The questions continued for over an hour. Andrew would be let down for short intervals only to be kicked and questioned further. Finally, he broke and confessed that he had been selling German Navy movements to the British Navy.

"Ha, you see?" the interrogator laughed, cracking his knuckles with satisfaction, "Pain will make a man sing like a bird. Thank you, Heiden. We really had no proof you were doing that. It was merely a hunch." The interrogator motioned to the guard at the vault like door.

By this time, Emily was trembling violently, and crying in fear and crushing grief. The mournful music added to the psychological damage.

The door opened and the guard pushed a metal frame device into the middle of the room. It was about five and half feet in height, and had a heavy wool covering. The interrogator walked to the sound hole and looked in at the cowering Emily. With a voice of pure evil, he laughed and said coldly, "This is what we do to traitors of the Reich. Please enjoy the show. Now commencing Act Two."

The curtain was closed for a few minutes, and then reopened like a curtain at a theatre. The interrogator motioned to the guard and said, "Take off the covering and prepare the prisoner." Emily's screams and pleading could be heard throughout the building as two guards wheeled the uncovered Fallbeil six feet from the observation window. The Fallbeil was the Nazi's version of the French Guillotine. Immediately four guards prepared Andrew for the final stage. He was screaming and struggling violently during the entire two-minute execution.

Emily stopped sobbing and watched through the window as two very tall men approached from either side of the execution room. They wore white business suits. Their hair was pure blond and they had a glow around them. Emily would later describe the next few minutes as being frozen in time as one of the tall men walked up to the sound hole and addressed her by name. "Don't be afraid, Emily," he said, "for we have come to take your father home to heaven."

"Angels!" whispered Emily.

With that, the safety on the Fallbeil was released. Emily tightly gripped her chest gasping for air. The last thing she remembers before fainting was the 16 inch 125 pound blade falling and seeing massive arterial spray cover the ceiling and sides of the tile-lined room.

Thus was Andrew Heiden's Home-going.

~ ~ ~

Emily was removed from the building into Peter's waiting car. Peter drove her home and helped her inside. Still feeling faint, she awoke to the smell of a fine Asbach brandy being wafted under her nose.

"Here. Drink this. You need it after that kind of ordeal." He was shaking and breathing heavily.

Emily weakly sat up and took a sip of the brandy. The alcohol burned as she swallowed, but it did calm her down a little.

"I'm done with the police force." said Peter, corking the brandy bottle.

"What do you mean?"

"I saw the whole thing. I won't support a government

which treats its citizens like that."

"Peter," she said, sighing deeply, "I will do anything I can to help the Jews and the Belguim Resistance, whatever it costs me."

Peter put his hand on her shoulder and said, "I will support you with my prayers, and will be silent if I am asked about your political views. But I can do no more."

"I know. Thank you, Peter." The two embraced and Peter left for the police department to turn in his gun and badge.

Chapter 2

GOD'S MESSENGERS

August 3rd, 1944
12:05 A.M.

After her father's execution, Emily had moved out of the hostel and into her childhood home. It was a warm night. A gentle breeze blew out of the south and lifted the curtains in Emily's room. She lay sound asleep in her bed when she was awakened by a knock at the door. She looked at her clock. It was just midnight. *Who would be at her door at that time of night?*

Her father had given her a 9mm Luger. He said he had found it in the forest in Eastern Poland. After discovering he worked for the British, she wondered if that was the whole story—not that it mattered to her.

She went to the drawer and took the gun with her to the door. "Who's there?" she asked, pressing her ear against the door.

"Help me," said a pleading voice.

She opened the door a crack and looked out, concealing the gun.

Leaning up against the railing was an old Jewish man in rags. She looked up and down the street. It was empty.

"Why have you come to me? You know the laws about helping Jews."

"I thought you might at least give me a cup of tea and a place to clean up before I leave Germany."

"Were you followed?"

"No. I am quite sure of that."

Emily hesitated for a moment considering the decision she was about to make. It is one thing to *say* she was going to help the Jews, and quite another to commit herself and really do it.

Then, as if another voice were speaking through her, she said, "Quickly, come inside."

Suddenly, the Jew was standing in her living room. The atmosphere was emotionally intense. She had broken a law that she knew could cost her life. There was no turning back now. Emily's heart pounded as she closed the door and looked at her illegal house guest.

The man was very thin with classic Jewish features. He looked at her with a contemplative smile, considering the bravery of this young lady.

"You know you have chosen to become a fellow sufferer

with us in this holocaust. Why did you let me inside?" he asked, sitting down on the couch.

"A year ago the Nazis tortured my father, then executed him with the Fallbeil. I was forced to watch the whole thing."

"I see. Thank you for your kindness. I will not take up much of your time. I leave for the city of Warsaw tomorrow."

"You can sleep in the spare bedroom. It's through here." Emily said, showing him the room.

The rest of the night went by quickly and soon morning came. She awoke to the aroma of strong French coffee. "Good morning," the old man greeted warmly.

"Good morning. Where did you get coffee?" asked Emily.

He smiled and poured her a generous cup. "I took it from a German. He was dead of course."

Emily smiled. The stranger's charm was irresistible.

"You know, it's all right to be afraid, Emily. Sometimes it can be a scary thing to step out in faith, and just give all to God who has promised never to leave you nor forsake you."

As he spoke, Emily's fear melted away. There was a calming presence about him.

The day wore on and Emily's college classes came and went. Something began to nag at her. *"How did he know her name? She had not introduced herself. Was he someone sent to spy on her, or just sent there by God—like the two angels that came to take her father to heaven?"*

Whatever the case may have been, she would never find out. When she arrived home, the stranger was gone. He had taken a few of her father's clothes, which made her smile. There on the table, she found a note that took her breath away. In a beautiful scroll hand, the note read, *"Be not forgetful to entertain strangers: for thereby some have entertained angels unawares."* (Hebrews 13:2)

Was this the reason she felt a strange warmth and peace when he spoke to her? Had she really given shelter to an angel that was perhaps just passing through on his way to another city? Whatever the case, she would keep the note for the rest of her life. She was sure it was written by a heavenly hand.

Chapter 3

SONGS FROM HEAVEN

The next day after school let out, Emily passed a young man and woman standing on the street corner. She didn't give them much thought until the young woman addressed her. "Beautiful day, is it not?"

Emily would later describe this greeting as a wave of energy that stopped her in the middle of the sidewalk. She turned and said, "Yes. I love this time of the year."

Both the young woman and man were over six feet tall, unusual for most Germans. The young man wore a comfortable dress shirt, woolen sweater and plain trousers. The young woman wore a green sweater and an attractive grey pencil skirt.

"You must be Emily." the young man said.

"Yes. How did you know?" asked Emily.

"I am Adam Fischer. This is my partner, Lydia Engle. We knew your father briefly. We met him in Eastern Poland when he was on a mission for the Resistance."

"How do you know so much about my father?"

"We're indirectly a part of the Resistance. Your father said you might be willing to put us up for a couple of days. We are heading to Warsaw on Sunday night."

"*Warsaw?*" Emily thought to herself. *"That's where the Jewish man said he was going."*

"All right," said Emily. "Yes, I have spare rooms in the house. It's not much, but it's shelter."

Emily led the way to the house and told her guests to make themselves at home.

Later that evening, Lydia sat down next to Emily on the sofa. Lydia asked her about her favorite church in Antwerp.

"Saint Paul's Church. I go there to pray sometimes."

"Do you ever sing?"

"Sing? I don't have much of a voice for that. After my father's execution I found that I didn't have enough joy to bring myself to sing." Emily put her head down, almost ashamed of her feelings.

"Emily, everyone in God's family has been given the gift of song, that they might sing to Him even in their darkest hour. Come. Why don't you show me Saint Paul's Church?" encouraged Lydia.

After a brisk, fifteen-minute walk, they arrived at the church. Adam, who had gone out earlier, was already inside admiring the architecture.

"Where have you been, Adam?" asked Lydia, pretending to be exasperated.

"I had to attend the passing of a young man at Breendonk," answered Adam.

Hearing the town's name hit Emily like a ton of bricks. She braced herself on a pew as her chest tightened. Vivid flashbacks of her father's torture and the crashing of the Fallbeil blade returned in an instant. She felt a strong hand on her shoulder. Her anxiety was instantly relieved. It was Lydia.

"Come," motioned Lydia, "Let me show you something up here." She led Emily up to the altar. Adam pointed to an ancient song page inside a large frame. The words were in Latin, done in beautiful colors. The lettering was in the classic Gothic.

Adam began to sing the words. *"Gaudeamus omnes in Domino...."*

"My, the acoustics in here are beautiful. Emily, do you sing at all?" asked Adam.

"I used to, a little. Haven't sung in about a year."

"And now you want to change that don't you?"

Emily was suddenly filled with joy and wanted to sing "Yes. I do want to change that."

"Let's start you out with something easy," said Adam, flipping through a hymnal. "Ah, here we go. Paul Gerhardt has some wonderful hymns." Adam had turned to Gerhardt's hymn entitled, "Why Should Cross and Trial Grieve Me?"

He started singing the first verse, and soon Lydia joined with the most perfect harmony Emily had ever heard. Lydia looked at Emily and smiled. As soon as she did, Emily found herself singing in beautiful harmony. When they were finished, Adam asked, "How do you feel now?"

"Like I'm on a cloud actually. It's amazing that five minutes of singing could make me feel that way."

Adam nodded and said, "Well, in times like these you need all the encouragement you can get. We'll do this again tomorrow before we leave."

As they were leaving the church, a young Jewish boy limped past. His clothes were bloodied and torn, and his face was filthy. Not wanting to draw attention to herself, Emily tried to ignore him.

"Hello, Moses," Lydia greeted warmly, taking out her handkerchief. She soaked it in the fountain next to her and cleaned his hands and face. As she helped the boy right on the public street, two off-duty Gestapo agents walked past.

They turned white with rage and asked her what she thought she was doing.

"Just helping a helpless child of the King," answered Lydia.

"Arrest her!" ordered one of the Gestapo agents addressing a local policeman walking by. Lydia stared at the agent coldly. So icy was her stare that Emily's blood ran cold for a minute. The policeman kept walking, and the agents simply shook their heads and left.

"God be with you, Moses," said Lydia warmly and handed him a piece of fresh bread from her pocket.

"What was that all about?" asked Emily, still confused why the agents and policeman walked away without a confrontation.

"We knew the boy's parents. They were killed by the Nazis last week. He's been homeless since then. Unfortunately, he's just one case out of millions of defenseless Jews being abused because of their race," explained Lydia.

They returned to the apartment pleased that they were able to help the young Jewish boy.

Emily had not slept well since her father's death. The emotional trauma had done something to her brain. She had continual flashbacks that penetrated her dreams. It had gotten so bad that she almost feared to sleep. Every time she fell asleep, she would be awakened by the sounds of her father's echoing screams. Late that night Emily got up and went to the kitchen and found that Lydia was up.

"Have you been having trouble sleeping?" asked Lydia, pouring a cup of red wine from the cupboard.

The question was a shock to Emily. How would this total stranger know that she was having trouble sleeping? "Yes I have. How did you know?"

"We know more about you than you think." Lydia gave her the cup and said, "Drink this, Emily."

Emily drank the contents and her eyes were immediately heavy. Lydia said, "It's all right.. You need to sleep. You must be prepared for the trials that await you. God is calling you to do something that requires physical and emotional strength." With that, Emily went to bed and fell into a deep, peaceful sleep. She slept without dreams until nine o'clock the next morning.

Emily awoke feeling like a new person. Lydia was downstairs preparing breakfast for her. There, sitting at the kitchen table, was the same Jewish boy that Lydia had helped the day before.

"This is one of your assignments, Emily," Lydia said, placing her hand on the boy's thin shoulder.

Emily was confused. "Moses is my assignment?"

"Yes, caring for one of God's people. Adam and I leave for

Warsaw at midnight."

"This sort of thing could cost me my life, Lydia!"

"I know. You will receive protection. Did you really think that God would call you into His service without being there for you the entire time?"

"No. I suppose not."

"Now, Adam and I have to go out for a little while. Do you think you can keep out of trouble while we're gone?" teased Lydia.

"Yes. I think so," said Emily with a smile.

While Emily stayed home with Moses, Lydia and Adam left on their own mission.

~ ~ ~

On an empty street in Warsaw, Lydia and Adam met with Abraham, the Jew who had been at Emily's home a few days earlier.

"You made it!" said Abraham, delighted.

"Yes. But we need to be back for tonight. We promised Emily we would sing with her one last time before moving on," said Adam.

"I see. As long as you are here by morning. That's all I ask. Handling thousands of people by myself might be difficult. How is Emily, by the way? She seemed to be such a nice and courageous girl, though troubled in spirit."

"She is a brave girl. She is at peace now. I don't think she'll be troubled by her father's death anymore. At least not for the remainder of the war. So, what is our plan? What are we doing now?" asked Adam.

"Himmler has ordered the extermination of tens of thousands of Jews. It begins tomorrow. It will be a rough start to the assignment. In one day there will be about 10,000 systematic deaths. The purpose of the operation is to crush the uprising in Warsaw. Come, I will show you one of the places of execution."

Abraham took Lydia and Adam to a steep railway embankment. "This is where the majority of the executions will take place starting tomorrow." He pointed to a spot at the bottom of the hill. "That is where the bodies will be burned."

"What's the purpose of all this horror?" asked Lydia.

"What's the purpose of this holocaust?" Abraham said, "We may never know the heart of men, killing millions of people because of their race, religion, for being mentally challenged, or for political reasons. The world may never understand the evil behind this holocaust."

Just then, a shot rang out, and an old Jewish man slumped

and tumbled down the embankment. The officer wiped the blood from his face and resumed his patrol. Their friend Daniel appeared and knelt by the old man. He said a few words over the body. A strong beam of golden light surrounded Daniel and the old man. Daniel took the old man to his heavenly home.

A few moments later, Daniel appeared again and approached Abraham, Lydia and Adam.. "I'll be glad when this war is over," he said.

"Daniel," said Abraham, "I'd like you to meet Lydia and Adam."

"Pleasure to meet you both."

"Daniel is stationed in Germany until the end of the war," said Abraham.

"Abraham, how did things work out with the young lady, Emily?" asked Daniel.

"She was a sad case. The Nazis tortured and executed her father and made her watch the whole thing as they played Chopin's Minute Waltz to add to the trauma."

"Rough. What movement?" asked Daniel.

"The Second."

"Oh, even worse. Poor girl. I was with her father at the very end after you talked with him in the cell. Philip and I took him home. He was so happy to see his Creator. I never get tired of seeing the look of their faces when they see the nail scars in His hands and feet. They just fall to their knees in worship. Makes my job worth every minute." said Daniel.

The four walked down the street and talked. "So, Himmler is getting more bold, is he?" said Abraham.

"Yes. Unfortunately for us. The next eight days are going to be especially difficult, but I'm quite sure the Father will be providing plenty of strength," said Daniel.

"I'm sorry to interrupt," said Lydia. "But we have to get back to Antwerp. We'll see you in the morning."

"Fair enough," said Daniel.

A few moments later, Adam and Lydia were in the city and knocked at Emily's door.

"Oh good. Your back," said Emily.

"Do you still want to go to the church tonight?" asked Lydia.

"Oh, yes I do."

"Well, we shouldn't waste any time then."

At the church, there were several people in the back rows, admiring the beauty of the sanctuary. "There are people here tonight," said Emily, feeling somewhat self-conscious.

"Well, don't be shy dear. Share the blessing of God with these people," said Lydia warmly.

Adam, Lydia and Emily walked together to the altar. They sang a hymn translated by Paul Gerhardt.

Lydia began at the fifth original verse,

"Now from thy cheeks has vanished
Their color once so fair;
From thy red lips is banished
The splendor that was there.
Grim death, with cruel rigor,
Has robbed thee of thy life;
Thus, thou hast lost thy vigor,
Thy strength in this sad strife."

Emily would soon find out these words were very appropriate. Verse after verse, the trio sang with angelic harmony. By the time they had finished singing the third song, "Veni, Veni. Emmanuel, there were over twenty people sitting in the pews. A total of seven ancient hymns were sung that night, each seeming to touch people's lives in a personal way. Finally, the performance was over, and it was time to go home.

As they had promised, Lydia and Adam left for Warsaw at midnight.

Chapter 4

WOLA MASSACRE

AUGUST 5th-12th 1944
Jewish residential district in Warsaw, Poland

The moon shone over the Ghetto in the early hours of August 5. As Daniel walked along the street, he saw the shape of a child laying in the street ahead of him. He walked up to the child and knelt beside him. "Jacob," Daniel said kindly, "It's time to go home." .

The starving eight year old boy weakly looked up and said, "I'm hungry. I want my daddy."

"I'm an angel, Jacob. God sent me here to take you to your new home in heaven. Your daddy is there."

"He is?"

"Yes. He's waiting for you. You've suffered enough," Daniel said softly.

Just then, Rabbi Friedman, one of the Torah Leaders in Warsaw, came quickly down the street. He recognized the boy and stopped beside him.

Daniel said, "Rabbi, it's too late for him. I've already taken him."

Friedman was frightened at Daniel's appearance. Daniel was dressed like anyone else in the Ghetto, but was shining from being in the presence of God.

"Rabbi, prepare your people. At dawn, over ten thousand residents here, especially women and children, will die today."

"Please! It can't be!"

"It's true, Friedman. A number of us have been assigned to this tragedy."

"Thank you for telling me." Friedman blinked his eyes, brushing away a tear. The reality of sin and his own mortality gripped him with fear and anticipation.

Daniel said, "Rabbi, if you confess with your mouth the Lord Jesus and believe in your heart that God raised Him from the dead, you shall be saved." (*Romans 10:9*)

He looked at Daniel. "But I am a Jew."

Daniel said, *"There is no difference between the Jew and the Greek: for the same Lord over all is rich unto all that call upon him. Whosoever shall call upon the name of the Lord shall be saved."* (Romans 10:12-13*)*

Rabbi Friedman instantly believed. He knelt and asked God to save him.

Friedman looked up to thank Daniel, but Daniel had vanished. The Rabbi was now filled with a peace he had never felt before.

Dawn came quickly. Just as the angel had said, the trucks of Russian and German soldiers began to roll down the filthy streets of the Wola district. The gun fire soon began from the windows and roofs of buildings, and the troops fired back.

The massacre had begun. Even though the Nazis experienced heavy fire from the Polish Resistance, the civilian casualties far outweighed military losses. Troops from the SS Sturmbrigadel were led by the infamous Oskir Dirlewanger. Thousands of the elderly, women and children were taken to Gorczewska Street and lined up along a portion of a steep railroad embankment and shot. At the end of the first day of the massacre, more than ten thousand people were executed.

For a week, angels worked tirelessly, escorting assigned people to their eternal home. Finally, on the twelfth day of the massacre, the smoke cleared, and nearly fifty thousand people had been killed. Members of the Polish underground walked through the Wola district capturing graphic photographs of this holocaust.

As the bodies were taken away and burnt, Daniel caught up with Lydia, Adam and Abraham..

"Daniel, finally it's over," said Abraham.

"Yes. I know. I've been assigned to accompany a little boy to Treblinka, and then back here to his family," said Adam.

"When?" asked Abraham.

"On the next train that arrives for deportation in two days. Lydia will be posing as one of the Jews headed for the camp. She will be the one who puts the boy on the train as it's leaving."

News of the massacre reached Antwerp in a couple days. Something in Emily's mind told her that the three unusual people that had visited her over the past few days were angels of death passing through on their way to the Wola district in Warsaw.

For some reason, she had been chosen to provide them with a place to rest. The three of them had left a residual peace behind which gave her strength for the trials that were ahead of her.

Chapter 5

RESISTANCE FIGHTERS

Anna Luther, Emily's childhood friend, was having trouble since aligning herself with the Belgium Resistance. Emily had been surprised to learn that Anna was involved in the movement, and also Anna's brother, Alec, who acted as a recruiter.

One evening as Anna and two of her friends were playing a game of cards, there was a heavy knock at the door. The girls looked at each other feeling the adrenaline course through their systems. Anna thought it must be the police about the supply truck she helped blow up by setting a mine on the road.

The girls quickly switched into offensive mode. Anna took her 9mm P-38 and slowly walked to the door. The other girls hid in the coat closet and watched while she answered the door.

Whoever it was at the door continued to knock.

Anna jacked a cartridge into the chamber and said, "Who is it?"

"Police. Open the door!" shouted an angry voice.

Anna concealed the pistol and motioned for the other girls to get ready. They quietly closed the closet door and prepared themselves for the confrontation.

"Sorry for the delay, Officer."

"No matter. Are you Fraulein Anna Luther?" asked the officer.

"Yes, I am Anna Luther. What is this about?" asked Anna, acting puzzled.

"We have orders to take you in for questioning about a supply truck that was blown up a few days ago," the officer replied.

Anna laughed nervously. "And you think I did that?"

"I just follow orders. Now grab a travel bag and come with us."

"All right. Come in for a minute while I pack a bag."

The officer along with two SS soldiers stepped inside and closed the door behind them.

As soon as Anna opened the closet door, there were silenced gun shots and then three heavy thuds on the floor. The two girls in the closet had guns ready to eliminate the problem.

"Come. Let's clean up this mess and get ready to move out. It's not going to take long for others to realize that something is wrong when the officer and soldiers do not bring me in for questioning," said Anna.

The girls quickly packed a bag and walked to the Ardennes Forest.

The Nazis used the forest's dense cover as the primary route in 1939 and 1940 to invade France. The Belgium Resistance also used the forest to do occasional espionage against German armored divisions. They moved silently through the forest avoiding checkpoints.

As Anna and her two friends neared one of the Resistance camps, they heard a noise in the bushes next to them. Anna reached for her gun. She stopped when she felt the barrel of a rifle pressing hard on the back of her neck.

"Don't move if you want to live," said a familiar voice in the darkness.

Anna turned slowly, recognizing a face in the moonlight. It was her brother, Alec. "Wow! That got my heart beating a little!" laughed Anna. She may have been a brave Resistance fighter, but deep down she was still just a girl.

"Sorry about that, but you can't be too careful. You never know who's going to be coming through," said Alec lowering his rifle. "I thought you were supposed to be coming later in the month."

"Well, we ran into some trouble when we got a visit from a police officer and two SS soldiers. But we took care of them."

"Come. I'll take you to the camp. You girls look as though you could use something hot to drink."

As the girls sipped the strong black coffee, they all discussed their thoughts on the Resistance with Alec.

"Alec, I think we really should bring in Emily Heiden to work with us," said Anna.

"Are you sure we can trust her?"

Anna said, "Her father was executed last year. Since then my contacts tell me she is taking care of a little Jewish boy in her home in Antwerp."

Alec nodded and said, "Okay. We will give her a chance. Get in touch with your contact in Antwerp and have her picked up. Make sure she is blindfolded when they get to the edge of the forest."

"All right."

"Remember. If she turns out to be a double agent, she dies. No questions asked," warned Alec.

"I understand."

"Well, you girls get some rest. We will be busy shortly working for the Resistance."

~ ~ ~

Meanwhile back in Antwerp, Emily slept soundly as a summer breeze blew across her face that night. She dreamed of the years before the war when her father would take her into the mountains to visit his friends who were farmers. The fragrance of the flowers that grew in the high meadows, and the hearty German fare wafted through her subconsciousness. Her dreams were interrupted by someone shaking her awake.

"Emily, quickly, get up!" said a male voice.

"What?" she asked, still groggy.

"I'm Max with the Belgium Resistance. You're not safe here. We can talk on the way, but we need to move quickly. Get the boy up and pack him a travel bag."

Something told Emily to do what Max said without question. She hurried to wake up Moses. "Quickly, get up," she whispered. We have to leave."

Five minutes later, they stepped out into the cool summer air and got into an old military jeep. Emily looked at her father's Braun pocket watch in the moonlight. It was 1:30 in the morning.

"Excuse me Max, but where are we going?"

"You will see. Actually, you won't see." said Max. With that he put a blindfold over her eyes.

An hour later, the jeep came to a stop and Emily was allowed to see again. They were surrounded by tall evergreens and hemlocks.

"Where are we?" asked Emily.

"The Ardennes forest. We will hike in from here." Max handed her a 9mm Steyr pistol and said, "I hope you know how to shoot."

"Yes I do know how to shoot, but will I need to?" asked Emily.

"You might In case we encounter Germans. They patrol this forest just as much as we do."

"Why the silencer?"

"We specialize in stealth. We certainly don't want to alert any German patrols in the area by the sound of gunshots," explained Max.

"I understand."

A few minutes later, the beams of jeep headlights appeared, accompanied by the rattling sound of a vehicle. "Quickly, get down!" said Max. He pulled her and Moses into the bushes and they dropped just in time to see a patrol jeep drive by, flashing a spotlight from side to side.

"Just let them pass. They don't know we're here. Lucky for them."

The jeep passed and Max led Emily and Moses deeper into the forest.

Soon the smell of smoke met Emily's nostrils. Emily thought the camp must be nearby.

Max gave a realistic bird whistle. A man in the bushes approached carrying a rifle.

"Max!" he greeted. "I've been expecting you. Is this the girl?"

"Yes."

"Thank you for bringing her."

"A pleasure to help."

The man handed Max a large gold SS ring and said, "I trust this will suffice as payment."

"Indeed, it does. Good evening." With that, Max hiked through the forest back to his jeep.

"What's your name?" asked the man. Dressed in military style clothes. He looked strong and confident as if he had already seen action working for the Resistance.

"I'm Emily Heiden and this is Moses."

"Welcome to the Belgium Resistance Emily."

The words resonated in her ears. For over a year, she had dreamed of fighting with the Resistance, but never thought that it would actually happen.

As they approached the camp Emily spotted Anna and the other girls.

Anna rose at the sight of her friend. "Emily, thank you for coming. Sorry for picking you up in the middle of the night, but you had done something highly illegal by hiding the boy. Your father worked for us, and the Gestapo watches the families of the Resistance far more than the average person. We knew you were in danger."

"What will happen to the boy now?" asked Emily.

"A contact will take the boy to a cabin on a lake in the mountains. The contact has an intense hatred for the Reich. The boy will be safe there until the end of the war."

"How do you know the boy will arrive safely in the mountains?"

"Because the contact who will take the boy was a sniper during the last war and hasn't lost his touch. And if the Germans are on the lake near the cabin where he and the boy will stay, they will be shot. He's got a boat in his shed near the shore if he needs to pursue a German boat."

"What do you want me to do now that I am here?" asked Emily.

"You'll be fighting with us for the Resistance. You can give justice to your father's memory."

Over the following weeks, the Belgium Resistance ambushed supply trucks, and stocked up on guns, ammunition and food which they brought to Resistance fighters in other parts of occupied territories. They also gave food to Jews in the ghettos.

Chapter 6

IT IS FINISHED

One beautiful afternoon after the war in 1949, Emily was shopping in a small village in Lauterbrunnen. In the heart of the market, she saw Peter and a group of monks talking and enjoying a mug of beer and thick cheese sandwiches. She slowly approached the table where the men sat.

"Peter!" she said smiling.

Peter turned his head at the familiar voice. "Emily, it has been a long time. How are you?"

"Pretty well."

"Excellent. Have you made peace about your father?" asked Peter.

"Yes. A long time ago. It still hurts sometimes, but I have peace about it now."

"Well, will you join us for some tea and sandwiches."

"Yes. That would be nice. You've changed, you know? You don't seem as outgoing as you were in the past," said Emily.

"Yes. I know." Peter said kindly. "I must be honest with you, I certainly did not approve of your years of revenge for your father's death by working for the Belgium Resistance. I did pray for you. But during that time, I became aware of my own sin and what God had sacrificed for my sin. I have devoted my life now serving my Lord and Saviour. I have joined the monastery here."

"Well, Peter. It is good that we both have found peace." said Emily.

"How's the tea," asked Peter.

"Delicious. What kind of beer are you enjoying?" asked Emily.

Peter and the other monks smiled. "We make it at the monastery. It's a traditional wheat beer, brewed with an array of different spices. Quite popular locally," explained Peter.

After chatting for an hour or so, Peter and Emily embraced and parted company.

For the rest of her life, Emily's telling of God's love and peace in the midst of sorrow filled the hearts of the hearers with joy. She recounted to family and friends the events that shaped her life: The pain and horror of her father's death; the heavenly singing ability she learned at Saint Paul's Church; and being chosen to offer a place to rest for three angels.

One day, Emily's son was looking through her jewelry box and discovered the note.

He read, *"Be not forgetful to entertain strangers: for thereby some have entertained angels unawares."*

"Mother, what is this?"

"Three of God's messengers stayed at my home in Antwerp. This is a note written by the first messenger. They were Angels of the Third Reich."

Das Ende

Made in the USA
Middletown, DE
08 November 2022

14199031R00108